Paula sighed. "You are more than generous."

MVFOL

"I can afford to be, especially if I sense that I can get a good return on my investment," Chase said seductively.

"And what exactly are you investing in?" Paula asked with more than a little curiosity.

He held her gaze. "How about a lady who appeals to me on multiple levels?"

Paula warmed. "That sounds tempting."

"I've also never been more serious," Chase said, continuing to look at her. "I think you're lovely, sexy, smart and obviously very talented."

"Don't stop now," Paula joked, though secretly she felt a wave of anticipation for what might come next.

"I won't."

Chase cupped her cheeks and, _____ perfectly, kissed Paula ten_____ his lower lip in her mout____ tongue, enjoying his taste ____ her mouth, she took in al___ their tongues danced whil_____ Chase wrapped his arms around her lower back, drawing them even closer without breaking their lip lock or the sexual tension in the air.

Books by Devon Vaughn Archer

Kimani Romance

Christmas Heat
Destined to Meet
Kissing the Man Next Door
Christmas Diamonds

Kimani Arabesque

Love Once Again

DEVON VAUGHN ARCHER

began writing mysteries in 2004, after a distinguished career as a nonfiction writer, by penning the legal thriller *Persuasive Evidence.* This was followed in 2005 by *Justice Served,* a finalist in the *Romantic Times BOOKreviews* Reviewers' Choice Awards, and in 2006 by *State's Evidence.*

Not content to rest on his laurels, Devon added romance fiction to his repertoire. In 2005, he began writing as Devon Vaughn Archer (previously R. Barri Flowers), and his novel *Dark and Dashing* appeared in the two-in-one collection *Slow Motion,* which received rave reviews and became a Black Expressions Book Club selection.

In 2006, Devon Vaughn Archer became the first man to write a contemporary romance for Harlequin's Kimani Arabesque line with the wonderful *Love Once Again.*

Devon has a BA and MS from Michigan State University, where he met his college sweetheart. They married seven months later. They currently live in the picturesque Pacific Northwest in Oregon, which Devon considers a natural setting for his romance and mystery novels.

He welcomes feedback from his fans and can be e-mailed at RBarri@RBarriFlowers.com. Learn more about his writing, book signings, contests and future releases on Devon's Web site at www.rbarriflowers.com. Also be sure to join his friends on MySpace at www.myspace.com/devonvaughnarcher.

Christmas DIAMONDS

DEVON VAUGHN ARCHER

KIMANI™
ROMANCE

If you purchased this book without a cover you should be aware
that this book is stolen property. It was reported as "unsold and
destroyed" to the publisher, and neither the author nor the
publisher has received any payment for this "stripped book."

To all my fans, and to the joy of love and romance at
Christmastime.

Also to Sleeping Beautiful and Maui Mermaid all
wrapped up in one special lady.

 KIMANI PRESS™

ISBN-13: 978-0-373-86139-2

CHRISTMAS DIAMONDS

Copyright © 2009 by R. Barri Flowers

Recycling programs
for this product may
not exist in your area.

All rights reserved. The reproduction, transmission or utilization
of this work in whole or in part in any form by any electronic, mechanical
or other means, now known or hereafter invented, including xerography,
photocopying and recording, or in any information storage or retrieval
system, is forbidden without written permission. For permission please
contact Kimani Press, Editorial Office, 233 Broadway, New York, NY
10279 U.S.A.

This is a work of fiction. Names, characters, places and incidents are
either the product of the author's imagination or are used fictitiously,
and any resemblance to actual persons, living or dead, business establishments,
events or locales is entirely coincidental.

® and TM are trademarks. Trademarks indicated with ® are registered in
the United States Patent and Trademark Office, the Canadian Trade Marks
Office and/or other countries.

www.kimanipress.com

Printed in U.S.A.

Dear Reader,

I would like to thank all of you for supporting my last two Kimani romances, *Kissing the Man Next Door* and *Destined to Meet.*

Now I am very excited to bring to you my latest contemporary romance, a holiday love story, *Christmas Diamonds.* As with my previous Kimani holiday romance, *Christmas Heat,* this one promises to tug at your heartstrings and make you fall in love with the protagonists, Paula Devine and Chase McCord.

Paula, an interior decorator, and Chase, a diamond jeweler and widower, turn chemistry into all-consuming passion as they navigate the waters between a professional and personal relationship. Over the festive Christmas season romance will carry them from Silver Moon, Washington, to the Diamond Capital of the World, Antwerp, Belgium, and back.

Paula secretly wishes to follow her grandmother's footsteps in being presented a diamond ring for Christmas.

The concept for this plot came from a bluesy Christmas song I have loved since childhood, "Merry Christmas, Baby" by Charles Brown. In it, getting a diamond ring for Christmas is likened to being in paradise. I tried to take that theme in carving out my holiday tale. I want my readers to take from this novel how wonderful falling in love can be when coupled with the joy of Christmastime.

I hope you enjoy reading *Christmas Diamonds* as much as I enjoyed writing it.

I am now at work on a new ultraromantic series, *Passions in Paradise,* with each story taking place on a different exotic Hawaiian Island.

And I also invite you to join my friends list on MySpace at www.myspace.com/devonvaughnarcher.

Yours truly,

Devon Vaughn Archer

Chapter 1

Paula Devine sipped her macchiato at the coffee shop, trying to ignore the intense sable eyes bearing down on her from the next table. The well-dressed, good-looking man had an enviable almond complexion and sideburns that merged with a thin mustache before meeting up nicely on his chin. He was obviously alone and perhaps hoping to hook up with whomever he set his sights on.

That would be her, given his apparent sole preoccupation. In another time and place, Paula might have entertained the thought of seeing what the man was made of. After all, she was naturally curious, like any single woman who was the object of a man's attention. Today, she merely wanted to finish her flavored latte and head to an appointment she had as an interior decorator.

"Don't you know it's not polite to stare?" Paula narrowed her tawny eyes at him, disregarding the fact that she was equally guilty. She couldn't help herself, all things considered.

His head snapped back as if he'd been in a trance. "My

apologies," he said, his voice deep and distinguished. "Guess I was totally entranced by your beauty."

Paula nearly laughed out loud, though she honestly felt flattered to some degree. Who wouldn't be? She'd gotten her fair share of compliments over the years. Most she had taken with a grain of salt, primarily because the smooth talker usually expected something in return. Often much more than was warranted. And since she wasn't offering anything—not this day or to this man—the words mostly came across as hollow.

"I'd say originality is not your strong suit," she told him candidly. "My advice to you is to find some new lines, then try them out on a woman who might actually be naive or desperate enough to fall for it."

He chuckled and ran his large hand through closely cropped, curly, raven hair. "You're probably right about the originality, but wrong on my intent. I wasn't trying to hit on you."

"Oh, really?" Her curly lashes fluttered with skepticism. "Why don't I believe you?"

His eyes widened. "Maybe because you're a little too full of yourself."

Paula arched a thin brow. "Excuse me?"

"I'm pretty sure you heard me loud and clear."

"I did," Paula acknowledged, wishing she hadn't. Now she had to tell him what she really thought. "Actually, it's more that I don't have the time or interest for silly games."

"Got it." He rose to his feet and buttoned the jacket of a three-piece gray windowpane suit that fit nicely on his tall, trim frame before lifting his still-steaming coffee. "Again, I'm sorry if I stepped on your toes."

Paula blinked and instinctively moved her toes inside her leather pumps. She imagined if he had stepped on them, she would surely have felt it. "Whatever," she said tartly, dismissing him with a look.

"Have a nice day," he told her politely. "And I mean that."

She watched him walk away with a confident strut and jutted

chin, half expecting that he might come back and plead his case. But he didn't, obviously deciding he couldn't be bothered.

Maybe I did have him pegged wrong. Or maybe not. Either way, the encounter had left Paula frustrated, and she had a pretty good idea why. She'd just gotten out of a relationship with a real charmer who was nearly as handsome as the one who had just vacated the premises. She wasn't quite ready to dive in headfirst again, only to find that the man was much more of a frog than a prince when all was said and done.

Besides, Paula had a feeling that man was already spoken for. She couldn't imagine someone so smooth and appealing to the eye not being taken. But that never seemed to stop men from checking out women and often playing on the attraction to see what they could get out of it. Perhaps he wasn't trying to hit on her, though she still had her doubts about that.

Glancing at her watch, Paula realized she'd let the time get away from her. *I can't be late. That would be too unprofessional.* She grabbed her bag and was out the door in a flash.

Chase McCord spilled some of his cappuccino on the sidewalk as he left the coffee shop on this cool, crisp October afternoon. He wanted to kick himself for that, much like when the lady caught him gazing at her perhaps a bit too long and had no problem telling him what she thought of it. The last thing he'd wanted was to have the woman think he was trying to get her naked and into bed before he even knew her name. Or knew if there was more to her than undeniably attractive physical qualities to go along with an attitude.

As it was, romance was not at the top of his agenda these days. Far from it. Not when the love of his life was no longer there to share his bedroom or anything else that mattered. It had been two years since Chase's wife, Rochelle, died. Though gone, she would never be forgotten. Not for one minute. He missed her so much and found it incredibly hard to engage in his professional pursuits without her subtle encouragement and unwavering companionship. But their time had come and gone, leaving him alone to make a life for himself.

Chase climbed inside his black Mercedes luxury car, started it and drove out of the crowded parking lot. He thought about the woman he'd locked eyes with a few minutes earlier, a lovely vision of her popping into his head. She was slender and gorgeous with smooth, honey-caramel skin that he'd almost wanted to reach over and touch. High cheekbones sat on a heart-shaped face, molding into a small nose and lips that were not too full and not too thin—just right. Her long, straight, blond hair was in a cool Sedu style.

The lady clearly had a poor opinion of men and was a bit too outspoken for his comfort. Not that any of it mattered at this point. He doubted they would ever cross paths again, which was certainly for the better as far as he was concerned.

His cell phone rang, and Chase turned his attention to it. "Hey," he said to Monica Rice, his best friend since college. She was an executive at McCord Diamonds, a chain of Pacific Northwest jewelry stores owned by Chase and his father that specialized in diamonds and other precious gemstones.

"Are you home right now?" she asked.

"No, but I'm on my way there. Why?"

"Don't forget to bring those insurance appraisals you took home yesterday when you come to the office."

"Oh, right," Chase said, glad she'd brought that up. "I've looked them over, and everything seems in order."

"Good." Monica paused as if distracted.

"Anything else?" he asked, suspecting she had more on her mind.

"Since you mentioned it, there are several new diamond consignments that need your approval pronto."

"I'll get right on it." He turned onto Orchard Lane. "Is that all?"

"For now." She laughed. "Just don't be too surprised if I have a lot more stuff that requires your attention before the day is through."

Chase chuckled. "Oh, I won't be. Comes with the territory." He didn't always like it, but overall felt he was in command of the situation and wouldn't complain. "See you soon."

"That's what they all say," she kidded. "Then I never hear from them again."

Chase reflected on Monica's merry-go-round of love interests, including three divorces and at least one engagement broken off. He couldn't imagine such in his life, as he took marriage commitment seriously.

"You'll get it right one of these days," he tried to assure her.

"Uh-huh. I'll believe it when I see it, or maybe I should say *him.*"

Chase smiled faintly. "Wish I could offer you some advice, but since my love life isn't exactly flourishing these days, I can only wish you the best of luck."

"You, too," Monica offered poignantly. "I know you haven't found a good match since Rochelle's death, but don't stop trying to find one. She's out there somewhere."

"I know," he muttered, imagining Rochelle scolding him for setting the bar too high in meeting a new woman to become the center of his life. The truth was, Rochelle was a hard act to follow, and, though Chase wasn't about to let the few women he had gone out with unsuccessfully dissuade him, he wouldn't settle for anyone less than he deserved.

Chase neared his house. Glancing at his dashboard clock, he noted it was a quarter to three, giving him a little time to work with before his meeting.

Paula got into her white Subaru Legacy sedan. She listened to her favorite Alicia Keys CD as she drove through Silver Moon, Washington, which was located nearly one hundred miles east of Seattle. She'd lived in Silver Moon since she was a child. The city was noted for its hospitality, laid-back lifestyle, clean parks and marvelous views of Mount Rainier.

Self-employed as an interior decorator, Paula had reached a comfortable point at this stage of her career. Due to the clientele she'd established, all of her appointments now came strictly by referral and word of mouth.

Such was the latest instance, in which a man had expressed an interest in having his great room modernized. She was always ready and willing to put her talents to work in beautifying any space, big or small. Satisfying her clients was not always easy, since individual tastes and needs varied. As long as she did her best every time, Paula was confident her clients would be happy and more than satisfied with the result, including the newest person to pursue her services.

She pulled up to the gated entry of the house. After identifying herself via the speaker, the gates opened. Paula drove around a circular driveway and parked behind a luxury vehicle. She got out and stood on a cobblestone pathway. Her burgundy pumps matched her designer business suit with a vented-cuff jacket and pants. One look at the house, and Paula was instantly impressed before even setting foot inside.

The multistory Georgian Colonial sat on a hill and was surrounded by western hemlocks. With a brick facade and white columns, it had paired chimneys, nine small windowpanes in each sash window and a beveled-glass front door.

Very nice. I can't wait to see the great room.

Paula stepped onto the porch and rang the bell. A moment later, the doors were opened by a fortysomething woman wearing a housekeeping dress.

"Hi, I'm Paula Devine," she said, trying to maintain her cool.

"Mr. McCord is expecting you. Come in."

Paula entered a ceramic-tiled entranceway, noting a hand-painted console table. Above it was a beautiful oil painting of yellow roses. She was led into a grand great room with a vaulted, wood-beamed ceiling and French-vanilla plaster walls. Two octagon olefin area rugs offset each other on the bamboo floor. There was a freestanding stone fireplace and custom-built walnut cabinetry. The window treatments were elegant swags and jabots.

As any interior decorator would do, Paula took it all in. For the most part, she liked what she saw.

"Mr. McCord will be right with you," the woman said. "Feel free to have a seat if you like."

"Thanks." Paula watched her walk away and then studied the furnishings. They were a combination of contemporary and traditional with floral fabrics and handcrafted accent pieces. In many respects it was as if she had stepped into a museum where everything was perfect, maybe too perfect for a room that should be open and fun.

I almost hate to sit down for fear of tarnishing the sofa.

She wandered over to the gourmet kitchen and found it just as impressive, with slate flooring, state-of-the-art appliances, including a Wolf range and glass-front Sub-Zero refrigerator, marble counters, a center island and a breakfast nook. If Paula had any complaint, it would have to be the orange walls, which seemed a bit outdated, and window treatments that failed to bring in enough light.

"Ms. Devine?"

The voice had a vaguely familiar ring to it. Paula turned around and saw the handsome man she'd encountered at the coffee shop. Her mouth dropped.

"You're—?"

"I'm afraid so." He looked equally surprised. Or perhaps somewhat amused. "Chase McCord."

Chapter 2

"I didn't realize at the coffee shop you were the person I had an appointment with—" Paula's soft voice broke, and she looked as if she wanted to run and hide.

"Would that have mattered?" Chase gazed down at the woman who had unjustly given him the cold shoulder. Again he was taken by her good looks, glowing oaklike complexion and the silky, flowing blond hair. He liked how her clothing fit snugly on her taut body. He caught a whiff of her perfume, a mixture of lavender and vanilla that was pleasing. "Or do you act differently toward potential clients than you do when meeting other men?"

She pursed her lips. "I try to treat all people the same way."

"Oh, really?" Chase raised a brow. "If that's how you treat *all* people, then—"

"Now wait just a minute," Paula said, coloring.

"Seems to me that once you make up your mind about someone, it's set in stone," Chase suggested.

She sucked in a deep breath. "I obviously misinterpreted things. If I offended you, I'm sorry."

"Are you?" Chase found himself uncharacteristically enjoying watching her grovel now that a job was clearly on the line. He supposed it was time to cut the lady some slack.

Her mouth opened slightly. "Look, why don't we just start over?"

"You think we should?"

Paula frowned. "Do you always respond to a question with a question?"

Chase chuckled. "No, not always. Only where it concerns business. I happen to judge people who work for me by how they present themselves."

She tensed. "I can assure you that you will find me the consummate professional."

Chase studied her and definitely liked what he saw. Apart from her obvious physical beauty, she was sexy as hell, though he suspected the lady was trying hard not to present that side of her while she was in business mode. As a man who had by and large put his profession first since he became a widower, Chase respected that much in the interior decorator. Nothing said they had to see eye to eye on a personal level, not to mention on a romantic and intimate level.

"Then let's start over," he told her.

Paula's lips curved upward at the corners. "I'm sure you won't regret it."

Chase liked the way she smiled, displaying straight, tight white teeth and dimpled cheeks. This notwithstanding, her work still had to stand on its own merits. He was not one to spend his hard-earned money frivolously, even if the interior decorator was extremely easy on the eyes.

"You come highly recommended," he noted.

She nodded. "Yes, your father, right?"

Chase grinned. "You did a nice job on his recreation room earlier this year."

"Thanks," Paula said sincerely. "It was fun turning the

room into a place where people could just relax and play games, leaving the outside world behind."

"I'd say you accomplished your objective." It was his father's favorite place to hang out at home. Chase also found himself spending a lot of time there playing pool and checkers.

Paula looked up at him. "You have a beautiful house, Mr. McCord."

"I'm pretty happy with it for the most part," he said. "And please, call me Chase."

"All right, Chase. And I prefer Paula."

He met her bold eyes. "So tell me what you think of this great room."

She took a sweeping glance and returned her gaze to him. "I think it's wonderful. Maybe a bit too pristine for my tastes, but it's certainly a room to admire."

"I've been told that often," he said. "My late wife chose everything you see in here. It was her passion to make this the dream house she'd envisioned."

Paula's brows lowered respectfully. "I'm sorry about your wife."

Chase felt her sincerity and also his own pain that resurfaced every time he went down memory lane. He pushed the issue away, not wanting to backpedal on the decision to redecorate he'd made for all the right reasons.

"She was a wonderful woman." His voice cracked with emotion. "Anyway, as much as I love this room, I think a change is definitely in order in here."

"Just how much of a change are we talking about?" Paula asked, her voice lifted a notch.

"I'd like a complete makeover. All of the current furnishings can be donated to a charitable organization." Chase faced Paula. "Do you think you could help me out?"

She grinned. "Yes, I'd love to."

"Great!" Chase said, grinning back at her.

"Is there any theme in particular that you're looking for?" she queried. "Perhaps one to complement the kitchen?"

"Not that I can think of," he admitted, having given it little thought other than wanting something different. "Rochelle, my late wife, gave each room its own individual style. Since you're the decorator, I'll trust you to use your discretion in here."

Paula's eyes lit up enthusiastically, and Chase could tell that ideas were beginning to form in her mind. That was exactly what he'd hoped for, as this was outside his area of expertise.

"Do you have a budget in mind?" she asked. "I certainly wouldn't presume that cost is no object, since it usually is with most people. I can pretty much work within any set amount you give me."

Chase appreciated her frankness, indicating her willingness to put the client first. This was in stark contrast to the woman he'd met at the coffee shop, who seemed to have a chip on her shoulder toward any man she felt had stepped over the line.

"Whatever it takes to get the job done satisfactorily," he said, knowing that his income afforded him the means. "Just draw up an estimate."

Paula nodded. "I'll put together a plan and run it by you. If you agree, we'll implement it."

Chase pulled out his card and handed it to her. "My home, work and cell numbers are all there."

She studied the card. "So you're in the diamond business like your father?"

"Yeah," he uttered proudly. "Seemed like a smart move after I graduated from college."

"I'm sure it was."

Chase wondered if she really believed that. The one thing he never wanted a woman to think was that he merely followed in his father's footsteps with no vision of his own. The truth was, he could have done anything with his MBA, but chose a dual major in gemology not only to keep the family business alive, but to put his stamp on it. He had done just that, and Chase had no doubt he'd taken the right career path.

Paula put his card in her wallet and took out hers. "Here's

all my contact info. Feel free to call me any time you have a question or concern about the project."

Chase thought it was unbelievable that an hour ago the same woman had no desire whatsoever to give him the time of day, much less her number. Now he had direct lines of communication with her and vice versa.

He stuck the card in his pocket. "I'll do that."

Paula dug in her purse. "I need to take some measurements and a few pictures of the room."

"Be my guest." Chase watched her methodically put a measuring tape to work and then use a digital camera to capture the room from different angles. Clearly she was in her element. He was as much fascinated with her body language as the process she went through to get a feel for the spatial dimensions and lighting. She moved gracefully and with an unassuming sexuality, making him almost wish he could just stand there and watch her all afternoon.

Paula turned to him. "Once I transfer these to my computer, I'll be able to play around with some different concepts until I find the one I think works best."

"I have no doubt you know what you're doing," Chase told her. "I'm looking forward to seeing the finished product." Even if that meant losing what Rochelle had poured her heart and soul into. Deep down inside, Chase believed that her efforts would never truly die and Rochelle's presence would be part of the house for as long as he lived there. With its great location and comfort, he saw no reason to move.

"I can't wait, either." Paula put away her camera and stuck out her arm. "I look forward to working with you."

Chase shook her hand, finding it very soft, warm and inviting. "Ditto for me."

He saw her out the door and couldn't help but think that it would be a good thing to have Paula here to spruce up his favorite room. This also meant they would have to get past their differences from the coffee shop and work in conjunction toward a common goal. She was obviously willing to meet him halfway, which was all he could ask for.

Chase went back inside and approached Jackie, the housekeeper he'd hired to come in three days a week to do the things Rochelle had once done. At first he'd tried to go it alone but quickly realized he was only making a bigger mess of things.

"Did you move the papers I had on the table?" he asked, knowing she sometimes went a little too far with her cleaning.

"I put them on your desk," Jackie said.

"Guess I should've checked there first." He scratched his chin. "I've hired Paula Devine to redecorate the great room. I'd like you to help her with anything she needs."

"Sure, I can do that."

"Thanks." Chase remembered there was something else he'd meant to tell her. "Also, I'd like that box of my late wife's clothes in the closet upstairs put in the storage room." He planned to soon donate them to charity, deciding it was time they were put to good use.

Paula couldn't believe her nearly rotten luck. Of all the men she could have spoken her mind to at the coffee shop, it had to be the very man she sought to hire her. One who happened to be quite well-to-do, judging by his abode and bloodline, and needed some work done to bring at least one room in his house up to snuff. Never mind the fact that in the looks department he could hold his own with the best-looking men on the planet: tall, definitely fit, with broad features and neatly trimmed facial hair that brought out his brown skin tone.

Thank goodness he didn't take my remarks too personally, or I would've really dug a hole for myself.

Her grandmother had always told Paula that she was a bit too frank for her own good at times.

And whom did I inherit that from?

Since the age of five, Paula had been raised by her grandmother and, in the process, had acquired Isabelle Devine's independent spirit and willingness to assert herself. Sometimes it got her into trouble, but more often than not, Paula was secure in being a strong woman who wouldn't be walked over or taken advantage of.

Paula supposed that the same spirit had been passed on to her mother, as well, who had left home as a teenager, making her way to several states before ending up in Atlanta. It was there that she'd gotten pregnant at twenty-one with Paula, raising her alone as a single mother. When times became too tough, Paula was sent to live with her grandmother. She became the only real mother Paula had ever known. Her contact with her birth mother had been infrequent.

She was proud to have her grandmother's spunk and would not apologize for it. On the contrary, Paula felt that being herself was the only way she could live. She only hoped that one day she would meet a man who could respect that without it being an affront to his manhood.

Paula drove home, happy that she had landed the job with Chase McCord. With an enormous great room, it would be a wonderful challenge to redecorate. The fact that Chase was allowing her to put her vision into it with little interference was an interior decorator's dream. She was intrigued by the man who was clearly more than just a handsome face with weak pickup lines that turned out to be not even that.

She wondered if he had dated anyone since his wife died. Or had the romance inside him died with her as if it had nowhere else to go? Paula knew something about that. She'd certainly had her fill of unworthy men who knew how to kill a romance. She had a feeling that someone like Chase McCord might be entirely different.

Paula arrived at the Prairie-style chalet where she lived with her grandmother. Built in the 1930s, it had been remodeled several times yet still retained its architectural charm and coziness. Paula loved the fact that her home was on a peaceful dead-end street, nestled amongst Douglas fir trees.

She went inside and immediately smelled collard greens. Since Paula's stomach was growling, she was eager to find out what else was for dinner. An excellent cook in her own right, Paula's grandmother had taught her well. Unfortunately, with her busy work schedule and often long hours, Paula rarely had time to cook anymore. That wasn't to say she couldn't find the time if preparing a feast for the right man.

Passing the sunken living room and formal dining room, Paula walked into the country-style kitchen. It had an eclectic feel, borrowing on the Colonial America and Old English Country styles. She saw her grandmother standing over the sink, peeling sweet potatoes for a pie while humming a song.

Isabelle Devine was seventy-one years old, but looked much younger. She was tall and lean with stylishly short, curled, silver hair and butterscotch skin. Isabelle had retired from the public school system five years ago after more than thirty years of teaching. Born in South Africa, she was classified under apartheid as "colored," reflecting her mixed-race sub-Saharan ancestry. Isabelle had been seventeen when her father brought his family to the United States to join him while he pursued his graduate studies in entomology at a university in the state of Washington.

It was there that Isabelle met Paula's grandfather, Earl Devine, a railway worker. They married a year later and had only been wed for six months when tragedy struck. Earl was killed in a railroad accident, leaving Isabelle a nineteen-year-old widow pregnant with Paula's mother, Jean.

It pained Paula that her mother had chosen to lead her life for the most part without reaching out to either her or Isabelle. Her grandmother and mother had not gotten along well, but Isabelle never stopped loving her only child to the point of selflessly rearing Paula as if she were her own.

Paula carried this weight on her shoulders, trying to compensate for her mother's absence in both of their lives by making Isabelle proud and never giving her cause to reject the role she had played in making Paula's life everything it was today. She wanted her grandmother to enjoy the years she had left as much as possible, and since she was in relatively good health for a woman her age, Paula was pretty confident Isabelle wasn't leaving any time soon, the good Lord willing.

"Hi, Isa," Paula said, using the nickname for her grandmother that she'd used for as long as she could remember.

"Hello." Isabelle stopped humming and offered a big smile. "I didn't hear you come in."

"That's me, quiet as a mouse," Paula said.

"You hungry?" Isabelle asked.

Paula moistened her lips. "Starving!"

Isabelle chuckled. "Well, I'll take care of that."

"Can I help?" Paula offered.

"No, just go freshen up. I won't be more than a few minutes."

"All right." Paula kissed her cheek and went upstairs. She had always been spoiled by her grandmother and couldn't imagine life without her.

Paula hoped that one day she would find the right man, someone who would enjoy spoiling her as much as she would enjoy being spoiled by him. The fact that she hadn't met him up to this point didn't mean he wasn't out there somewhere. He could be right around the corner just waiting to run into her.

She stepped inside her bedroom that was well down the hall from her grandmother's room, with two spare rooms in between to give them some needed privacy. In redesigning her personal space, Paula had done the walls in soft apricot, added plantation shutters to the windows and installed lush gray carpeting. Decorative accents complemented hand-carved mahogany furnishings. She sat for a moment on the antique bed, where silk taffeta hung above the headboard to form a crown canopy.

Paula suddenly found herself curious about Chase's bedroom. In light of the rooms she'd seen at his home, she assumed his bedroom was spacious and immaculate. If things worked out right, maybe he would allow her to redecorate it, as well. Or would that be overstepping the boundaries of his late wife's memory a bit too much in Chase's mind?

After freshening up, Paula went downstairs for dinner. She sat at the dining-room table across from her grandmother.

"So how did the prospective client work out today?" Isabelle gave her a curious look.

Paula bit into a biscuit. "I got the job."

"Wonderful."

"I hope he agrees when I'm done," Paula said sincerely.

Isabelle cocked a brow. "He?"

"Yes, *he.*" Paula chuckled, knowing her grandmother's propensity to try to get her hitched to any single, good-looking, gainfully employed and available man.

"Remind me again what the job is," Isabelle said.

"Redecorating his great room."

Isabelle lifted her glass. "Oh, yes. Sounds like something right up your alley."

"I think I'm up to the challenge."

"And when have you ever not been?" Isabelle tossed out.

Paula smiled. "You give me way too much credit."

"You've earned it," Isabelle said sincerely. "How old is your client?"

"I'm guessing he's in his midthirties," Paula answered, which would put him a few years over her age of thirty-one.

"That's perfect, if I say so myself." Isabelle favored her with a scheming look. "So, is he single?"

"He's a widower." Paula couldn't begin to imagine losing a significant other so young in life. How on earth did one manage to go on after that? She hoped she would never have to find out.

"Then he and I have something in common besides you," Isabelle said.

"That's true. You both lost your spouse at a young age."

Isabelle closed her eyes for a moment. "You never really get over it, no matter how much time passes."

Paula reached across the table and touched her grandmother's hand. "I know." She watched a shadow of sadness cross Isabelle's face like a shadow. Paula had seen that look many times before. She wished things had been different for Isa. In spite of being an attractive woman of color and seeing men off and on over the years, her grandmother had chosen not to remarry, believing that no one could ever take the place of her beloved husband, Earl.

Paula wondered if Chase felt the same way about his late wife. Had he deemed her irreplaceable, no matter who else might enter his life? Or maybe he had moved on but simply was looking to find the right woman to occupy his time.

"Is he handsome?" Isabelle wiped her mouth with a napkin.

"Yes, very," Paula admitted, blushing at the thought.

"Does he have any children?"

The question had crossed Paula's mind, too. "Not that I know of." She had seen no signs to that effect at his house. "But he does have a housekeeper, if that counts for anything."

"Not as offspring," Isabelle said with a chuckle. "But it does indicate a desire to keep the house clean, and that's a good sign since there's apparently no one to help in that regard."

"I was thinking the same thing," Paula told her honestly. "I've also met his father."

"Oh?"

"Yes, Sylvester McCord. You remember I worked on his recreation room."

Isabelle's eyes widened. "You mean the gentleman in the diamond business?"

Paula nodded. "That's the one."

"What about his son?" Isabelle asked inquisitively.

"What about him?"

"What's his profession?"

"He works with his father," Paula responded. She could tell by the look in Isa's eyes where this was going.

Isabelle tilted her head. "Hmm… So maybe this is someone you should get to know personally."

Paula looked at her thoughtfully. "I'm not sure either of us wants to go there, especially after I sort of put him off when we met earlier today by chance."

"I doubt he'll hold that against you," Isabelle said. "If he did, he wouldn't have hired you."

"Point taken." Paula tasted her diet drink. "Still, ours is a professional relationship, and I don't want to mess that up."

Isabelle narrowed her eyes. "You mean like with your last beau?"

She colored. "Kind of."

The thought left a sour taste in Paula's mouth. Things between her and Sheldon Burke had started off with a bang and much promise, but in the end it was obvious that he wasn't the right man for her. She saw no reason to go down that road again too soon, even if Chase seemed like every woman's dream from what little she knew and had seen of him.

"Don't let one bad apple taint the entire tree," Isabelle said, leaning forward. "Maybe it was a sign when he hired you."

Paula knew her grandmother was big on signs and karma and all that, dating back to her youth in Johannesburg. But she didn't share this belief, preferring to think that destiny was something you controlled rather than the other way around.

Still, she went along with it up to a point. "I guess I can accept that, just like any job I get might be in the cards, or should I say stars?"

Isabelle smiled. "There could be much more here for you than a job. The man seems to have the right foundation. If he has any common sense, he'll realize you're one good catch."

"You would say that," Paula said, expecting nothing less from the woman who always saw the best in her.

"I know what I'm talking about," Isabelle said candidly. "Besides, it's just as easy to marry a wealthy, handsome, lonely man as it is one who is poor and not so attractive."

Paula's eyes widened. "Who says he's lonely?"

"Who says he's not?" Isabelle retorted. "There's only one way to find out."

Paula chuckled. "What am I going to do with you?"

"I'm not the one you need to worry about, sweetheart." Isabelle held up her hand, sporting a diamond wedding ring. "I already have my ring. Earl saw to that before he ran into harm's way, leaving me something very special to remember him by."

Paula marveled at the ring with tiny diamonds that still sparkled. She'd heard the story a thousand times about how her grandfather worked the railways tirelessly like so many others of his day and died doing what he needed for his family. But not before he'd expressed his deep love for Isa by giving her a diamond engagement ring for Christmas, following it up with the wedding ring the next summer.

Paula never tired of the wonderful tale. Indeed, it had been her wish since childhood to find that type of all-consuming, powerful love from a man who would give her a diamond ring at Christmas—or any other time of year—setting the stage for a lifetime of marital bliss. She wasn't sure it would ever happen, even if her grandmother seemed to believe it was only a matter of time. Finding a man she wanted to spend the rest of her life with had proven elusive thus far for Paula.

She certainly wasn't ready to say that Chase McCord could turn out to be her Prince Charming. And since he'd already found true love once, he probably wasn't looking to get married again, particularly not to someone who had already let him know she wasn't interested in him romantically. But things had changed since their initial meeting, hadn't they?

For now, Paula just wanted to focus on giving his great room the type of makeover that would give Chase more than his money's worth. If anything else happened between them, she was open to crossing that bridge once they got to it.

Chapter 3

Chase entered the offices of McCord Diamonds, Inc., located in a new business complex in downtown Silver Moon. The interior decorator he'd hired was still on his mind. He admired her enthusiasm for the job. Her attractiveness was a bonus, even if it certainly wasn't a prerequisite for giving his great room a makeover. As a man who had always appreciated female beauty and had been without such in his life since his wife died, Chase couldn't help but be intrigued by Paula in spite of her earlier brush off.

He greeted the receptionist, Celeste, and headed for his office before Monica Rice intercepted him.

"There you are," she said.

"Yeah, right on time," he joked, eyeing the thirty-six-year-old with gold-rimmed glasses and a brunette half updo. He handed her a folder. "Here are those insurance appraisals."

"Thanks." Monica gave the contents a cursory look. "No problems, then?"

"None that I saw."

"Good." She frowned. "Unfortunately we do have a problem with the new gemologist we hired for the West Slope store."

Chase raised an eyebrow. "What's the problem?"

"He's more interested in hitting on me than designing jewelry."

Chase chuckled. "Are you sure you're not misinterpreting his intent?"

Monica pursed her lips into a pout. "I think I know a come-on when I see it, Chase."

He recalled that Paula had thought the same thing about him earlier today without justification. What was up with women jumping the gun over a simple look of admiration? Wasn't that part of the point of being attractive and put together? That didn't mean the gemologist hadn't stepped over the line and their zero-tolerance policy on sexual harassment.

"I'll talk to him," Chase told her.

"Not necessary," she said succinctly. "I think I can handle Mr. Zachary Lockhard."

Chase caught the glint in her eye, suggesting to him that she was not entirely unresponsive to the man's interest. Might even be another marriage in the making for his good friend. Maybe he should warn Mr. Zachary Lockhard to leave her alone or be prepared for a walk down the aisle.

"Well, be sure to keep me posted." Chase glanced at the closed door to his father's office. "Is Dad in?"

Monica scoffed. "Where else would he be?"

"Right." His father was even more of a workaholic than he'd become since Rochelle's death. Chase had little incentive now to step away from the business, with no social life to speak of other than a few dates that went nowhere. He hoped that would change someday. "I'd better bring him up to speed on a few things."

Chase knocked once on the door, pausing a moment before opening it. His father was talking animatedly on the phone and waved him in.

Sylvester McCord was sixty-five, thirty years Chase's

senior. Tall and slender, his receding hair was gray, matching his deep eyes. As always, he wore an expensive suit, befitting his position as head of the company.

As president of McCord Diamonds, Chase was happy to be a part of something his father started from scratch and built into a very successful enterprise. He had visions of one day expanding to other states and even abroad. Chase sat across from his father's large desk, thinking briefly about the redecorating project in his home that signaled a new beginning as he tried to get his personal life back on track.

Sylvester hung up and smiled at his son. "We're getting in a new line of fine jewelry."

Chase nodded. "Yes, that's good. We'll update our catalog accordingly and reach out to those looking for more than just diamond engagement rings and wedding bands."

"My feelings precisely. But never overlook what will always be at the core of our business." Sylvester flashed him a serious look. "People who are getting married depend on us to help them find the perfect rings to signify their bond of love."

"Of course." Chase glanced at the finger where his wedding band had been. He'd decided a few months ago that it was time to remove it, though he would always treasure the ring as a keepsake of his love for Rochelle.

"It's almost time for you to head to Antwerp," Sylvester said, eyeing him. "Are you ready for it?"

One to two times a year, Chase went to Antwerp, Belgium, known as the diamond capital of the world. As a member of the Independent Jewelers Association, he would make the trek to purchase diamonds for their stores and also act as a diamond broker for select customers.

"I'm always up for the trip," Chase responded. It was true— though not as much as when Rochelle had been alive. They had always taken advantage of the opportunity to enjoy Antwerp as a romantic getaway. The last two times he'd gone, he'd been there alone and had felt totally miserable, reminded with each place he visited of her and the memories they'd created.

"That's what I like to hear." Sylvester leaned back in his chair. "By the way, how did the meeting go this afternoon with the interior decorator?"

"Good. She's hired."

"I thought she might win you over." His father smiled. "She'll do a great job."

"I'm sure she will," Chase said pensively.

"In fact, you might want to keep her around to redecorate the whole house."

Chase lowered his brows. "I'm not sure I'm ready to take away everything Rochelle put her blood, sweat and tears into."

"You'll never take it away from inside you, son." Sylvester put a fist to his chest. "It doesn't mean you love her any less if the house is redecorated to represent that you're moving on with life, like Rochelle would have wanted you to do."

"I know." Chase sighed. "I just want to take one room at a time and see how it goes."

"That's understandable." Sylvester drummed his fingers on his desk pad. "So, what did you think of Paula?"

"She seems professional enough," Chase said nonchalantly.

"Beyond that," Sylvester probed.

"What do you mean?"

Sylvester grinned. "How did you like her as a woman?"

Chase chuckled uneasily. "Did you recommend her to date, or to redecorate my great room?"

"Both," he said candidly. "If she can get it done for you on both counts, then that's even better."

"Dad, don't." Chase decided it was best to stop this train in its tracks in spite of his father's good intentions.

Sylvester displayed a look of disappointment. "What? She's a pretty lady, and you're a chip off the old block when it comes to being urbane, educated and handsome. I just thought that if you two met, well…you could both help each other in more ways than one."

"Thanks, but I'm okay right now on my own," Chase clarified.

"I don't doubt that for a minute. But you need more than just being okay. Having a woman in your life again who you can be serious about would make it worthwhile in ways that this business could never achieve, no matter the success."

Chase couldn't deny that he often felt empty and lonely. A woman's touch that meant something was one of the things he missed most about Rochelle, along with the camaraderie found in a loving relationship. But Paula? Yes, she was certainly the type of woman he was attracted to physically. But her character was a whole different matter.

"Paula and I aren't on the same wavelength when it comes to romance," he voiced straightforwardly. Or was he being presumptuous?

Sylvester gazed at him with a cocked brow. "How can you be so sure?"

Chase stiffened. "We had a run-in beforehand, and clearly there were some issues."

"Since when have you ever shied away from a challenge?" Sylvester asked.

"I'm not shying away from anything," Chase said with a defensive edge to his tone. "I'd rather not confuse business with my personal life right now."

"Okay, I get it. You can't blame the old man for trying to do right by his son, can you?"

Chase smiled, happy to have him there for guidance and support. "No, I can't."

"You'll find someone out there sooner or later to make your life complete again," Sylvester told him confidently. "I did, and I couldn't be happier."

Chase had been just twelve years old when his mother was killed in a car accident. It was the first time death had really hit home for him. Losing someone he loved so much so early in life had been painful. His father, devastated, as well, had remained single for years before meeting Evelyn, a divorcée. They hit it off right away, had a whirlwind romance and tied the knot.

While Chase was pleased with his father's choice in a partner to share his life, he wasn't sure he'd be as fortunate. Rochelle had meant everything to him. Though he had no problem with dating women, having someone step into her shoes as a lover, confidante and maybe even wife and mother someday was hard to contemplate at the moment. But that didn't mean he was totally opposed to the idea, either, if such a lady should materialize. Chase thought about Paula Devine in that regard, even though he knew very little about her aside from the fact that she was an attractive interior decorator and didn't appear to have much interest in him as a man. Maybe they had both overreacted when they met and just needed time to figure out how they felt.

A week had passed since Paula last saw Chase. During that time, she'd used the photos and measurements she'd taken to study the layout of his great room and had put together what she believed to be a fantastic decor scheme. Paula stood at the door to his home with nervous enthusiasm, as was often the case when she was about to make a presentation.

When Chase opened the door, she noticed that he was wearing a dark designer suit that enhanced his suave good looks. He smelled really good, too.

"Nice to see you again, Paula," he said smoothly.

"You, too." She flashed her teeth under the heat of his gaze.

"Come on in."

Paula followed him inside to the great room. She was keyed up and thoughtful about her plan of action. She hoped Chase would love her ideas and embrace her vision for the room.

Chase faced her. "Can I get you something to drink? There's water, wine, punch, orange juice… You name it."

"Nothing for now, thank you," she told him. "Maybe I'll have something after the presentation."

"Okay, why don't we sit down, then?"

Paula joined Chase at a cluster of chairs with a small table before them, setting her briefcase to the side. "I really admire the way your wife decorated this room," Paula said honestly. "It has a great ambiance."

"I appreciate that." Chase's chin jutted. "I know she would have been thrilled to hear it, too."

Paula imagined they might have been friends had the opportunity presented itself, but obviously that would never happen. She would never get to know the woman who had given her love to the man Paula sat next to, but he was someone that she could become better acquainted with, even if strictly on a professional level.

"I hope you'll like my idea for the room as much as I do," she told him evenly.

Chase clasped his hands. "It'll be interesting to see what you've come up with."

Paula laid her briefcase on the floor, opened it and confidently removed a sketch she'd created. She handed it to him, having already memorized each and every detail.

"First of all, I think the furniture should be arranged in a way that provides a more welcoming, lively environment rather than merely functional."

"Hmm…" he said, studying the sketch.

"I think we should replace the chairs we're sitting in with taupe leather chairs and replace this table with a pedestal cocktail table." Paula stood up, moving toward the sofa and loveseat, feeling as though she had his full attention. "I'd like to swap these with a chenille sectional and bring in a new curved, glass-top coffee table with storage drawers, primavera end tables and Tiffany table lamps."

"Sounds good," Chase said, gazing at her.

Paula was encouraged by his reaction. "I believe adding a half-round pine curio near the entrance, a collage of artwork for that high wall and two Caribbean area rugs would complement the furnishings nicely," she said. "I would finish things off by replacing the window treatments with linen-pleated window shades."

Chase grinned. "Wow! Your suggestions are really creative. I'm impressed."

Paula resisted a smile. "That's nice of you to say, but this is my job, and I take it very seriously."

"As you should."

He met her eyes, making Paula feel warm inside. *Better keep my mind on the issue at hand. I hope I can say the same for him.*

She walked back to her briefcase and got out the cost estimate, handing it to Chase. "If you want to make any adjustments, it's completely negotiable."

Chase flipped through the two pages, giving them a quick glance. "It's fine."

"Great." Paula thought about sitting back down, but wasn't sure if she should get too comfortable. At least not before she'd turned her plan into reality.

Chase stood up. "So, how long will it take to get all this done?"

"Well, I'll need to meet with my contractor and arrange for purchase and delivery of the furniture along with the removal of your current pieces," Paula said thoughtfully. "If everything goes according to the plan, I'd say that your new great room should be ready in about ten days or so."

He stepped closer to her. "I think I can wait till then."

She studied his handsome face, sensing mixed emotions about changing a room his late wife had created. "If you have any reservations about the layout or items chosen, we can always make the adjustments," Paula felt compelled to say.

"That sounds more than fair." Chase looked down at Paula. "I can see why my dad recommended you."

She lifted an eyebrow. "Oh, really?"

"You're nothing if not thorough. I like that."

"It comes with the service," she told him. "I'm sure you'd find that to be true with any reputable decorator."

"I'll take your word for it," he said. "Finding an interior decorator who looks as nice as you might be much more difficult."

Paula blushed. "Are you flirting with me?"

"Maybe I am a little. I'm also being honest." Chase kept a straight face. "But I don't mean to make you uncomfortable— again."

"You're not," she was quick to say. In fact, Paula found herself feeling quite comfortable around him, which was part of the problem. It would probably be a mistake if either of them crossed any boundaries. Or would it be more of a mistake to avoid the obvious chemistry between them? "I really appreciate the compliment. I just think it's best if we keep this a professional relationship."

Chase lifted his hands as if blocking a blow. "Hey, it was just a compliment, Paula. Nothing more, nothing less."

Paula felt foolish. For the second time, she had jumped the gun and misinterpreted his compliment as something more. She blamed her reaction on her unstable and disappointing history with men. They had made a habit of making her feel very special, only to reveal later that they fell far short of what had been advertised. She somehow doubted that would ever be true with Chase.

"Sorry, it's just me, not you," she explained, hoping it would be enough.

Chase furrowed his brow. "He must have done a quite a number on you."

Paula sighed. "You must be a mind reader."

"Not really," he said. "It's obvious you have a chip on your shoulder. I figured someone must have left it there."

She wanted to open up to him, but felt this wasn't the time or place. Maybe she would if they got to know each other better down the line. "Let's just say the last man I was involved with made me want to run and hide from all men," Paula said with an uneasy chuckle.

Chase tilted his head, and, for a moment, Paula thought he might kiss her. She wasn't quite sure how she would react if he did. Instead, he took a step back.

"I'm sorry to hear that," he said genuinely.

Paula blinked. "I'll get over it in time."

"I hope so. One jerk shouldn't represent the entire male species."

She smiled. "I agree."

His eyes crinkled. "I'm glad to see that we can agree on something where it concerns the ups and downs of the dating world."

"So am I," she told him.

Paula could tell that Chase wasn't just another good-looking man on the prowl. There was obviously far more depth to him than that. Had her grandmother been right that maybe their meeting was a sign? Or did they both have the type of history that would only complicate any chance for moving beyond decorator and client?

Chase saw Paula out and once more scolded himself for being attracted to the lady he'd hired to do his great room. He couldn't help but feel this way even if reluctant to give in to his emotions. Though she bore some resemblance to Rochelle, it was more than that. Her poise captivated him, along with the softness of Paula's voice behind those luscious lips. Her lithe body movement dripped with sexuality and had him imagining what it would be like to make love to Paula.

It had been a long time since anyone had aroused Chase mentally and sexually. He wasn't sure if this was a good thing or not. Paula seemed to want to keep things strictly professional between them, and a part of Chase felt the same way. Maybe it was too soon to start a relationship with someone else. Rochelle was gone, but her presence was still very much with him and in this house where they had created and shared such wonderful memories.

Chase stood in the great room, looking around as if for the last time. He liked the makeover plans Paula had shown him and was ready to see them implemented. Hard as it was, he needed to do this for closure and moving beyond Rochelle and what she meant to him. He was sure she would want him to move on with his life and be happy. Beyond changes to his house, Chase wondered if it was time to really start working on finding someone to give his heart to. The thought of being in a serious romance again sent sensations up and down his spine. He had a lot of love and affection built up inside him and wanted more than anything to find an extraspecial lady he could share that with. Maybe a smart and sexy woman like Paula Devine.

Chapter 4

Divine Decor and Designs was located on LaGrande Drive amidst a collection of other suites offering home and garden renovations. Paula sat at her desk, taking a sweeping gaze at the large office that included a showroom, window displays and some of the latest ideas for interior decoration. She'd designed the place herself, wanting it to represent her vision along with being an artistic, fun place to visit.

She phoned her contractor, Bradford Stowe. They had worked together for the past year, and she was pleased with his amazing ability to get practically any job done in a timely manner. His team of an architect, electrician and muscle was perfect for her needs.

"Hey, Paula," he said in the gruff voice of a man pushing sixty. "I was just about to take out the trash before my wife has a conniption. What's up?"

"I've been hired to redecorate a great room," she told him. "The work mostly entails putting in new furnishings and taking out the old ones. The swags and jabots will need to be replaced with window shades."

"Sounds simple enough."

"Will you be able to get your crew together on Wednesday morning?" Paula asked hopefully.

Bradford cleared his throat. "Not a problem."

"Great. My client is eager to see the room transformed to fit his needs."

"I'm sure you won't disappoint, and neither will we," Bradford responded.

"I know I can always count on you," Paula said and meant it, never underestimating the importance of a good crew.

"Haven't had any complaints yet, knock on wood," he indicated. "I'll try to keep it that way."

Paula could say the same thing, by and large. Her work spoke for itself, and many of her clients came back for additional redecoration projects, which in her mind was the highest form of flattery. She recalled that Chase's Dad, Sylvester McCord, had indicated that he might want her to give his patio a face-lift. Paula welcomed the opportunity to put her talents to good use for him again. For the moment, though, her focus was on his son and achieving the objectives set forth.

A few minutes later, Paula answered a call from her grandmother.

"Are you busy?" Isabelle asked.

Had it been anyone else, Paula would have said yes, as she was in the process of working on her next assignment. But she always tried to find time for the one person who had been there for her through thick and thin.

"Not really," Paula said. "Is everything okay?"

"Just fine, child," Isabelle reassured her. "I wanted to check and see how your latest meeting went with the diamond man."

Paula smiled. Honestly, they seemed to click, at least professionally speaking. There also appeared to be the potential for something more, as she felt there was some chemistry between them. Of course, she couldn't get too carried away daydreaming about a man she barely knew, even if it seemed like Isa practically already had their future together laid out.

"It went well," Paula said. "Chase loves the design scheme I came up with."

"Did you think for one minute that he wouldn't?" Isabelle asked, confidence brimming in her voice.

"You never know for sure. Not everyone thinks I walk on water like you, Isa."

"Just wait till he gets to know you better. I'm sure you'll have the man eating out of your hands."

"I think I'll settle for having him fall in love with my work," Paula said with a chuckle, definitely not wanting to prematurely think in terms of strong romantic possibilities between them. "Besides, we haven't reached the stage of dining and feeding each other yet."

Isabelle laughed. "Give it time."

Paula rolled her eyes. She had plenty of time to regret her last relationship. And even the one before that.

"Whatever happens will happen," Paula said nonchalantly.

"Sometimes you have to make things happen," Isabelle countered. "The good ones can't always read your mind."

"And how would you know what's on my mind concerning the good ones?" Paula was curious.

"I'm not so old that I've forgotten how nice it is when you actually connect with someone special."

"And who says I've made such a connection?" Paula asked.

"Not all things have to be in words, child," Isabelle told her wisely. "A feeling can be just as powerful."

Paula felt there was no winning this round with her grandmother, even if she found no fault in her argument. "I'll try to keep that in mind."

"Good. I'm happy to hear it."

Paula peeked at her watch. "I hate to cut this short, but I've got a few things I need to finish up."

"I won't keep you any longer. Oh, by the way, if you could pick up my prescription on the way home, I'd really appreciate it." Isabelle took medicine for an elevated cholesterol level.

"Consider it done," Paula told her.

"You're a dear."

"And who do you think I inherited that from?" Paula teased.

"I wouldn't know," Isabelle said jokingly.

"Oh, yes, you do," Paula shot back merrily. "I love you, Isa."

She disconnected and counted her blessings, starting with having Isa as a grandmother and confidante. Then there was her interior-decorating business, which allowed Paula to use her college education and creativity productively. All that was missing was a man who could light up her life with his intellect and humor, not to mention his skills in the bedroom. When would she find that man?

Paula's mind drifted to Chase, wondering if the sparks she was starting to feel between them were only her imagination or could possibly be something much more tangible.

Chase worked out of his home office while his great room was being refurbished. He tried to focus on ordering gems for the stores. Aside from diamonds, the company did well with emeralds, opals, pearls, sapphires and tanzanites. It would soon be the holiday season, which was normally their busiest time of the year.

Chase mused about modernizing part of his house as second thoughts crept in. Maybe he should have kept things as Rochelle had created. Would making some drastic changes mean he was erasing memories of her? The last thing he wanted was to negate what they had built together. He quickly rejected the idea, knowing that this wasn't about tearing down barriers to the past, but rather building bridges toward the future. It was time he quit making excuses for living in yesteryear and got on with his life. Giving the great room a new look was a step in the right direction. Whatever came next in his redecorating scheme, if anything, he was prepared to take it head-on.

"I think maybe we should add some onyx and jade," Monica suggested over the phone.

"Uh, yeah, that's a good idea," Chase mumbled.

"You're sure? You sound distracted," Monica said.

Chase stopped musing and gave her his full attention. "Yes, we're both on the same page," he said. "You always make sound business decisions, Monica."

"I try my best. If it's good for the company, I say let's go for it."

Chase leaned back in his chair. "Agreed."

"So how's the great-room project going?" Monica asked.

"Good, I think. I've kind of buried myself in the office so I wouldn't be in the way." Or maybe it was that he couldn't bear to witness them taking away little pieces of him in the process, in spite of his better side recognizing it was a sound decision.

"You know Rochelle would be the first one to say you probably should've done this a long time ago, right?"

"Yeah, I could see that," Chase acknowledged, knowing she hadn't been one to dwell on things out of her control.

"Then don't stress out about it."

"I'm not," Chase said unconvincingly.

"Remember, I know you better than most," Monica said. "I'm sure you're reminiscing and wondering if everything in that house should remain untouched for all time as a tribute to your life with Rochelle."

Chase sighed. "So maybe I am a little. Can you blame me?"

"No, but it doesn't do you any good to hold on to something that only exists in your heart."

"Is that a bad thing?" he questioned.

"Of course not," Monica told him. "Keeping a special place for Rochelle is important. It's equally important to move past that place when you still have the better part of your life ahead of you. And that includes laying out a new course on your house."

"You've made your point," Chase conceded.

She smiled. "That's why I hang around, to keep you grounded," she joked.

"And you do your job well," Chase acknowledged. The one thing he could count on from Monica was straight talk, which he greatly appreciated to help put his life in a proper perspective. In fact, he had already begun to come to terms with letting go of the past and focusing more on what possibilities the future held over and beyond remodeling his personal space.

After hanging up, Chase watched Paula walk into the office. She was sharply dressed in a black sweater and gray plaid skirt with slingback flats. He couldn't help but admire her as a striking woman, stirring a fire deep within his soul.

"Hi," she said. "We've wrapped up your great room and just need your approval now."

"All right." He got up from his desk and moved up to her. "This should be interesting."

Paula laughed softly. "As long as that translates into your liking the result."

I like you, and that's a good start, Chase mused, even if their affiliation was strictly professional. It didn't mean that couldn't change over the course of time. He was certainly open to the possibility.

His lips curved into a smile. "Let's take a look at your work."

Chase felt some anxiety at what he might see when he rounded the corner of the curved hallway. As far as he was concerned, there was no turning back. He just hoped he didn't live to regret his decision to redecorate.

The first thing Chase noticed upon entering the great room was the chenille sectional and rounded glass-top coffee table. He eyed the primavera end tables and Tiffany lamps, then shifted his gaze to the smartly arranged taupe leather chairs and pedestal cocktail table. The half-round pine curio fit nicely, and an arrangement of artwork seemed perfectly suited to the room. He glanced at the Caribbean rug beneath his feet and then the new window treatments before settling his eyes on the interior decorator.

"Well, what do you think?" Paula looked at him expectantly, while her crew also waited to hear his opinion.

It took Chase a moment or two to adjust to the changes in the great room, so stark were the differences. But there was no doubt in his mind that this had been the right decision. "I absolutely love it!" he declared.

"That's a relief." Paula took a breath, eliciting chuckles from everyone.

"Good job." Chase grinned at her. "Your sketch didn't do proper justice to this very nice transformation."

"I'm glad you like it," Paula said, offering a toothy smile.

Chase pinched his nose. "I think the room suits me well and will be perfect for get-togethers."

"I was picturing the same thing," Paula told him.

"I guess we were on the same wavelength without even realizing it," he suggested.

She nodded. "Looks that way."

"We're done here, then?" asked Bradford, the contractor.

"I think so." Paula regarded Chase. "If there's anything you'd like rearranged, we're happy to do it."

Chase scanned the room again, looking for an excuse to change something. He couldn't find one. He was certain that Rochelle would have approved, too. "Wouldn't change a thing," he said positively.

"Then our mission is complete," Paula told her team. "Everyone can go about their business till we meet again."

Chase watched Paula show them out the door before she returned, leaving them alone. Whether he wanted to admit it or not, he felt good when he was with her.

"Would you like to have a glass of wine to celebrate a job well done?" he asked.

She beamed, licking her lips. "Sure, I'd love one."

Paula was delighted to have gained another satisfied client, especially this particular client. She never took her work for granted or felt confident that repeat business was a given. She certainly hoped for another opportunity to do more redecorating for Chase in the future.

At the moment, Paula welcomed the offer to have a drink with Chase, if only to spend more time with him. She admired him in a polo sweater and slacks as they stood in his kitchen. This was the first time she had seen him dressed casually, and the image definitely agreed with her.

"Here you go," Chase said, handing her a goblet of red wine.

She smiled. "Thank you."

He sipped his wine, gazing at her. "Have you always had an eye for interior decoration?"

"I suppose I have to one degree or another," she said. "I was pretty good way back in the day at making my bedroom the coolest place to hang out with my girlfriends."

Chase nodded thoughtfully. "I'm sure they were envious."

Paula chuckled. "I think it was more about who had the best clothes and most outrageous hairstyles back then."

"Yeah, I know a little something about that," Chase said humorously. "At least regarding clothes."

"I can imagine you would, since you obviously have a good sense of style," Paula said, aware that fashion sense didn't simply come with the territory.

"I've got another room I'd like you to take a look at," he told her, "if you have the time…."

Paula jumped at the opportunity. "I'd be happy to." She had nothing important on her agenda this afternoon. And she definitely didn't have anyone waiting in the wings to share an intimate moment with. She suspected the same was true for him.

Paula followed Chase up a spiral staircase and down a hallway before entering…

"It's the master suite," Chase said coolly. "I was thinking that you could work your magic in here."

Paula felt a prickle of heat as she realized his words could be interpreted in more ways than one. "Oh, really?" she asked mischievously. "And what sort of magic are you talking about?"

Chase tossed his head back with laughter. "Well, I wasn't thinking in terms of mystical powers," he said. "But I'm definitely interested in seeing what ideas you have for renovating this room."

Paula met his peering eyes, causing her heart to flutter and her temperature to rise. She quickly turned her attention to the room, hoping to focus on something less dangerous to her emotions than the man himself.

Chapter 5

Paula surveyed the massive bedroom with its U-shaped layout. It had floor-to-ceiling windows and a double tray ceiling. A tile fireplace with gas logs made the sitting room cozy. The master suite's furnishings were Edwardian, in floral patterns and prints. She noted a large walk-in closet and an adjacent, luxurious bathroom.

"What do you think?" Chase asked, his gaze angled down at Paula's face.

"It's beautiful," she responded. There was no other way to put it. Paula eyed the elegant four-poster bed. "Your wife had good taste."

"That's what everyone said." He took a couple of steps on the plush carpeting and looked around. "Rochelle would be the first one to tell me that I need to change things."

"Really?" Paula was surprised. She wasn't convinced that any woman would encourage her husband to give his bedroom a makeover once she was gone.

"Sure." Chase mused. "That's how she was, never one to live in the past."

"I see," Paula said enviously. She wondered if she could ever be so selfless in her love for a man if her death came prematurely. "What do you think she would suggest?"

Chase gave the question some thought. "I'd say probably something more masculine."

"I agree," admitted Paula.

He grinned. "Guess good minds think alike."

"I guess so."

She immediately began to envision some changes she could make to suit him. Perhaps something not *too* masculine, so he would still be comfortable enjoying the room with a female companion. Paula impulsively thought of herself, imagining what they could do together in his bedroom.

"I'd like you to redecorate the master suite," Chase told her firmly.

Paula's eyes lit with enthusiasm. "I'd be glad to," she said. She was more than up for the challenge.

Chase grinned. "Excellent! Based on the standard you set with the great room, I'm sure you'll come up with something equally spectacular in here."

She colored. "You're very good for my ego."

"All the credit goes to you," he insisted. "What's that old saying… 'The proof is in the pudding.' I'd say you've earned any accolades that come your way."

"Thank you for that," she said, slightly overwhelmed by the ease in which he made her feel so special. "Actually, I'm glad you've hired me again. It might be nice to hang around you a little more."

Chase met her eyes with clear interest. "Oh, really?"

"Yes." She maintained her courage in spite of the heat emanating from his gaze. "Who knows what I might learn about you?"

He laughed heartily. "That's true, and you might get to

uncover all my secrets. And I just might learn one or two of yours."

She grinned. "Anything's possible."

Paula realized that they had somehow gotten close enough to kiss. She had a notion that his lips would feel good on hers. Very good. Was he thinking the same thing? For an instant, she wanted to let herself go and make the first move. Why not show a bit of daring? Most men seemed to like that. Was Chase one of those men? Paula held back the urge, fearing it might send the wrong signal at the wrong time.

She took a step back, doubting his feelings for her. "If you want, we can talk about it over dinner in a couple of days, after I get a chance to put together a plan."

"Dinner sounds good." Chase put his hand in his pocket, never taking his eyes off her. "Your place or mine?"

She smiled, flattered that he was trying to tempt her with tantalizing words.

"Actually, I was thinking of a restaurant," Paula answered. "Are you familiar with Aspen's?"

"Yes, I've been there a few times."

"How about six o'clock on Friday?" Paula asked.

"Six is fine."

Her cheeks rose. "Then it's settled. I'll see you then."

"I look forward to it," he said equably.

Paula suddenly felt it was getting a bit stuffy in the room. Or was it because her heart was suddenly beating so rapidly in the presence of such an enticing man? She took out her tape measure, hoping to take her mind off Chase, knowing that would be all but impossible. "Okay, I'll just take some measurements of the room and be on my way," she said quietly.

Chase half grinned. "Take your time. I'll be downstairs if you need me."

Paula watched him leave the room before exhaling and steadying herself. *Focus, girl, on something more under your control than Chase McCord.*

She moved around the master suite, taking measurements

and making notes. Near the bed, Paula spotted a framed photograph of Chase and an attractive lady. They were holding hands and beaming. *His wife,* Paula thought. It felt a little creepy, as if she were encroaching on a dead woman's territory. Paula quickly dismissed the notion. People passed on all the time, and the world didn't end. Chase had decided to move on; she was there to redecorate.

Still, Paula couldn't help but be more than a little intrigued by the prospect of being in his bed, sensing a sexual vibe between them. She had a feeling their intimacy would be incredible. But that was all a fantasy right now. She sighed and put away her notes.

Chase had really wanted to kiss Paula yesterday. Apart from the fact that he hadn't quite gotten over his grief for Rochelle, Paula was working for him. That had to come first, as he didn't want to stand between her and the redecorating that was giving his house a needed uplift. After all, that was the whole purpose of their involvement, despite his father's intentions.

However, Chase couldn't disregard that he was turned on by Paula and could sense her attraction to him. Could their mutual attraction move to the next level?

The bell ringing snapped Chase out of his reverie and back to the real world. He used the remote to turn off the TV and headed toward the foyer. Chase opened the door and saw his father and stepmother. He had invited them over to check out the new great room.

"Hey," Chase said with a big grin. "Come on in."

"Hey, son." Sylvester smiled, patting him on the shoulder as he walked by.

"How are you this evening?" his stepmother asked.

Chase kissed her cheek. "I'm good."

Evelyn McCord was petite and had a short brown perm. Chase had come to love her as though she were his birth mother. Evelyn had been there through his formative years, helping Chase's father keep him on the straight and narrow.

"I can't wait to see what you've done to your great room," Evelyn said anxiously.

"You'll be surprised," he told her as they rounded the corner.

Evelyn's eyes widened. "Wow. It looks wonderful."

"You really like it?" Chase asked, knowing that not everyone saw eye to eye on room decor.

"Yes, the interior decorator did a marvelous job," she declared.

Chase smiled and looked at his father. "What do you think, Dad?"

Sylvester ran a hand the length of his chin. "It's like a totally different room. She did a hell of a nice job."

"I think so, too," Chase concurred.

"I told you Paula was very good at what she did," Sylvester said. "Everyone who sees my recreation room falls in love with it and wants to know who redecorated it."

"You're preaching to the choir," Chase said. "In fact, I've hired Paula to redo my bedroom next."

Evelyn cocked a brow. "Your bedroom? Really?"

Chase suddenly felt uncomfortable. "Well, it seemed like a good idea to try something new," he explained.

"I think it's an excellent idea," Sylvester said encouragingly. "Your room could use some sprucing up."

"Your father's right," Evelyn chimed in. "Paula clearly knows her stuff. You might as well tap into her great talent and see where it takes you."

Chase liked the sound of that. He imagined Paula's talents went much further than redecorating. Maybe he would find out firsthand how much further.

"He sounds like a real catch," said Paula's best friend, Virginia Kensit.

They were jogging in the park near Paula's house. She hadn't meant to go overboard in her description of Chase as totally masculine and the kind of man she could easily fall head over heels for. Still, she felt she had understated just how wonderful the man was.

"He is," Paula admitted dreamily. "But we're not dating."

"You already said that." Virginia, a couple of inches taller and maybe too thin in Paula's mind, ran her hand through damp yarn braids. "I know you're *only* working on Mr. Hottie's house. It's a mere formality."

"What's with you and Isa?" Paula chuckled nervously. "You're both always looking for something that isn't there. Not yet, anyway."

"That's not what I'm reading between the lines." Virginia caught her breath. "Go ahead—tell me how you really feel about him."

She isn't going to let up, Paula thought. She decided there was no sense ducking the issue. Since she had started it, she might as well finish it.

"Yes, Chase is very good-looking and more," she said candidly. "But he's also a widower who still keeps a photo of his late wife on a bedroom table."

Virginia rolled her eyes. "So what?"

"So maybe he's still hung up on her," Paula suggested, going against her own beliefs deep down inside. "What if he always will be?"

Virginia frowned. "That's perfectly normal when you've lost a loved one. It doesn't mean he hasn't already moved on—especially if he has a good enough reason to," she hinted.

Paula sighed, wondering if she could be that good reason. She got the impression Chase was interested in her, but to what extent over and beyond physical attraction and loneliness? She was more than most men could handle as an intelligent, successful, ambitious and beautiful woman of color who wanted—demanded—a man who had similar qualities and would treat her with the utmost respect and be willing to meet her at least halfway on any issue of contention. In her past adult relationships, the men had fallen short of these standards in one way or another at the end of the day. She wasn't always faultless, but owned up to being less than perfect while trying to better herself as a woman and a romantic mate. Paula believed that Chase held the qualities that were most attractive to her, now that she'd gotten to spend some time with him. But it was still too soon to know if the strong vibes passing between them could turn into a relationship or not.

"We'll see what happens," she told Virginia. "Right now, it's all about giving my client everything he's paying me for."

"You've already been there, done that, girlfriend. What's more important now is what you're willing to give the man for free."

Paula laughed while keeping pace. "You're wicked, girl." She knew that Virginia juggled men the way a circus performer did bowling pins. But that didn't necessarily make her an expert on men and successful relationships.

"Hey, I'm just being candid," Virginia said unblinkingly. "You deserve a man who will wait on you hand and foot and doesn't ask for an arm and a leg in return."

Paula wrinkled her nose. "Those are a lot of body parts to keep track of, girlfriend. I'd rather he focused at least part of the time on my mind—something that wasn't the case often enough in some past relationships, as far as I was concerned." She certainly had no problem with a man who wanted her body as much as she wanted his, as long as he still appreciated her intelligence.

"Give the man a chance," Virginia urged her. "Don't assume Chase is anything like Sheldon, heaven forbid, or even Johnny, for that matter."

Paula would just as soon forget about her last two boyfriends. Neither had the qualities she wanted for a long-term involvement. Johnny was too unstable, and Sheldon failed to keep her interested enough. Chase certainly appeared to be cut from an entirely different cloth.

"I'm not assuming anything," Paula said, feeling the strain

in her legs. "Chase and I are still a work in progress, much like his house. Let's just see how things go."

"Sure, whatever you say," Virginia said, rolling her eyes.

Chase felt a little jittery as he waited in the restaurant's lobby for Paula to show up. Though he'd gone out on several dates since becoming a widower, no woman had quite captured his fancy the way Paula had. Apart from a good work ethic and physical attractiveness, he liked her style. She was definitely a smart lady and candid in her thoughts. He wanted to go deeper into who she was as a person and how she got to that point. He wondered how Paula felt about moving their relationship beyond employer and client. Something—perhaps the ease with which they related to one another—told him she was as open to the possibility as he was.

"Hello there…"

Chase looked up and saw Paula come from behind another waiting patron. "Hi," he said, admiring the beauty she made seem so natural. A gray skirt suit fit well on her slim frame and showed off her nice legs. The briefcase she held firmly reminded him that this was simply a business meeting.

"Sorry I'm a bit late, but I was delayed by a prospective client," Paula said and took a breath.

"It's fine." Chase smiled at her and imagined she probably had clients lined up to take advantage of her talent. "Shall we go in?"

She nodded. "Yes, I'm famished."

They sat at a window table in the corner and ordered white wine.

"Do you come here a lot?" Chase asked curiously, gazing at Paula over the menu.

"Only when my budget allows," she said candidly. "I recommended it because it's close to where we both live and quiet enough to talk without being drowned out by other patrons."

"Well, it was a good choice, whatever your reasons." Chase had been there once with Rochelle and another time with

Monica. Both times, he'd enjoyed himself and thought the food was great. He wondered if Paula had dinner at nice restaurants with other clients, or had he been singled out as more worthy of such an occasion? Chase found himself equally inquisitive about who she spent time with socially or otherwise.

"Thank you." Paula closed her menu. "I love their broiled salmon with Dijon mustard!"

"Sounds tasty," Chase said.

"Believe me, it is."

Chase grinned. "In that case, I'll follow your lead and give the salmon a try, along with a bowl of clam chowder to start things off."

"Good choice. I'll have the same," she told him.

After ordering, Paula set her briefcase on the table. "I'm sure you're wondering what ideas I came up with for your room."

"The thought had crossed my mind," Chase told her drily, sipping his wine. He tried to picture what direction she would take this time and how it would differ from Rochelle's approach. "What have you got for me?"

Paula removed a sketch and handed it to him. "We start off with a rearrangement of furniture that I believe will create a more natural flow to the room and allow the sun to shine favorably on you when you're in the sitting room, or maybe reading in bed."

Chase studied the sketch with interest. "I like it." Though he never read in bed, he did appreciate the sunlight pouring into the room, brightening it and therefore making it more cheery.

"To that effect, I would like to replace the heavy drapes on the windows with cellular shades," Paula told him. "They're not only energy efficient, but will absorb sound and complement the wall coloring."

Chase nodded. "Go right ahead and put in the shades." At this point, he was open to any suggestions that would give the room a new identity while still maintaining its integrity.

"Now let's talk about the furniture." Paula reached back into the briefcase and pulled out a couple of photographs, passing them to him. "I think a satinwood, bow-front Georgian chest and dresser set like you see in the top photo would be perfect for the room. This would be complemented by a Maltese entertainment cabinet that's shown in the second photo."

Chase grinned favorably. "Very nice."

"Glad you like it." She paused, took a sip of wine and lifted another photograph from her briefcase. "As the centerpiece of the room, I think you should have a Louis XV hand-carved-walnut king bed with patterned leather insets like this," she said, pointing at the picture.

"Wow." Chase studied the picture. "It's beautiful."

"I think so, too," Paula agreed. "And I'd like to add some fluffy pillows along with a quilted duvet cover or a double-woven embossed bedspread."

"Sounds good to me."

Chase imagined himself in the bed with her, surrounded by fluffy pillows, making passionate love like two people who couldn't get enough of one another. A wave of intense desire swept over him, and he wondered if Paula might be thinking the same thing. Surely he wasn't the only one getting aroused and excited at the mere notion of being naked and engaged in hot, sensual, unbridled sex.

Their clam chowder arrived, quickly stemming Chase's libido as he turned his attention to the food.

Chapter 6

Paula tried hard to keep her mind off Chase, but found it to be utterly impossible. He was simply too suave in a navy suit, and his mouth, wide and ultrasexy, seemed tailor-made for kissing. The idea of their lips joined together in rhythmic smooching gave her carnal thoughts that went far beyond a kiss. She imagined them slowly and methodically removing each other's clothes, pausing with each piece to take pleasure in every inch of their bodies, his lips leaving a burning trail down her quivering body until they united as one like love-starved intimates eager to please.

Feeling her temperature rise and her body tremble with desire, Paula quickly pushed away the vivid images. She managed to refocus on her meal and wrapped up her presentation on refurnishing the master suite in Chase's home.

"I think putting less formal rattan furniture in the sitting-room area is a great idea," Chase said while dabbing his mouth with a napkin. "You really do know your stuff."

Paula blushed. "I try to turn each room into something that truly embodies the client's persona."

"Well, so far you've really hit the mark on my persona to bring out the best in the space." Chase crinkled his eyes at her. "My dad was quite impressed with the great room."

Paula smiled graciously. "That's nice to hear." She remembered being slightly intimidated by Sylvester McCord, sensing that he would be a hard one to please. Instead, he had been very open-minded and a great client to work for, just as his son was turning out to be. "Are you and your father pretty close?" she asked Chase, curious.

"Yeah, we're tight," he responded. "I can pretty much talk to him about anything, and he'll actually listen."

"That's wonderful." Paula lifted her fork, ruminating. "What about your mother?"

Chase paused. "The woman you met at my dad's house is my stepmother. My real mother died when I was twelve."

Paula felt badly for him. "That must have been hard."

"Yeah, it was." He absently moved the food around his plate. "Car accident."

Paula gasped. "I'm so sorry."

"For a while there it seemed like just a bad dream, and she would walk through the front door as though nothing had happened. But…she never did." Chase choked back emotion. "Anyway, that was a long time ago. And I understand now that it was just her time."

Paula blinked. "I suppose you're right, sad as that is."

"But my stepmother has been just like a mother to me," Chase added.

"That's good to know," Paula said.

Chase ate a piece of salmon. "What about your parents?"

"I never knew my father," Paula said, wishing it weren't true. "My mother sent me to live with my grandmother when I was five. We don't see each other much these days."

This was one of Paula's biggest regrets—not having her birth mother around to share the ups and downs of life with.

But it wasn't her choice. Her mother had decided she couldn't handle raising a child on her own and had found someone else to take the responsibility.

Chase's brow furrowed. "Wow. Where's your mother now?"

"The last I heard, she was living with a man in the Bahamas."

"I'm sure you've struggled with her decision making. Losing a mother to tragedy is one thing, but if she's still alive yet mostly absent from your life…"

Paula stiffened. "I stopped feeling sorry for myself a long time ago. We all do what we have to do for whatever reason. I've just had to deal with it and move on with my life."

"Is your grandmother still alive?" Chase asked.

"Yes, thank goodness." Paula smiled at the thought. "She's seventy-one years old and still has a lot of spunk. Isa has been my rock over the years."

"Well, that's good." Chase reached for a slice of bread. "Everyone needs such a person in their life."

"That's true." Paula felt they were both fortunate in that regard, as his father obviously filled this role in Chase's life. But what about his romantic life? She sensed there was no one serious there right now, meaning he was on the market. So was she. The notion excited Paula. As did learning more about the handsome man before her.

"So tell me about the diamond business?" she asked with fascination.

Chase gazed at her. "What do you want to know about it?"

"Well, what is it that you do, exactly? I mean, in terms a layperson can understand."

Chase leaned back thoughtfully in his chair. "As president of the company, I do a little bit of everything. I purchase diamonds and other gemstones, advise clients, promote the company, do a little design work and more."

"Sounds impressive."

Chase chuckled. "No big deal, really. I just do my job like anyone else."

"Have you done any other type of work?" Paula asked curiously.

"In college, I worked at the front desk in my dorm, put in some all-nighters at a local grocery store and even did a little bartending."

"Hmm, so I imagine you were probably pretty good at getting those college girls drunk?" Paula teased.

He chuckled. "Well, I usually knew when they reached their limit even if they didn't."

"Good answer." She liked him better all the time.

Chase smiled. "I've been a jeweler ever since the good old days," he told her.

"It obviously agrees with you."

"I'm happy with my job most of the time," Chase said.

"Your dad must be proud of you," Paula speculated.

Chase nodded. "Yeah, I guess he is. He doesn't exactly pat me on the back every other day for a job well done, but we both seem to be on the same wavelength when it comes to running the company."

"That's great."

"Not to say that we don't have our disagreements from time to time," Chase said evenly. "It usually comes down to who can be the most stubborn."

"Sounds a lot like me and my grandmother," Paula confessed.

Chase grinned. "I know we're both smart enough to let them win most of the time."

"Exactly," she agreed.

As Chase refilled their wineglasses, Paula sensed he was a man who knew how to take charge on a date. Not that she considered this a date. Or maybe it was, now that they had concluded their business and she had given him the estimate of costs. Paula realized that she enjoyed spending time with Chase whatever the purpose. He seemed to feel the same way.

Chase gazed at Paula over the rim of his glass. "So, how did you turn a girl's dream into professional success as an interior decorator?"

"Through sheer determination and a good talking to by my grandmother," she had to admit.

"That may be, but I think you left out one thing," Chase suggested.

Paula's eyes widened. "What?"

He gave her a straight look. "Talent. You really know how to arrange and decorate a room so everything flows naturally. That's something you can't teach. It has to come from within."

"Keep that up and I'm going to really get bigheaded," she said, only half joking.

Chase laughed. "I doubt that. Something tells me you have both feet on the ground as much as I do."

That was a compliment Paula was happy to accept. It also told her more about the man and how he took his success in stride, which was a quality she appreciated. She was excited at the prospect of getting to know Chase better.

"I think you're right about that," she said, her voice betraying the common philosophy.

"Tell me something I don't know." He spoke with assurance.

Paula chuckled. "Well, I happen to be a big Motown fan. I love all those great artists like the Four Tops, Temptations, Supremes, Mary Wells, Marvin Gaye, Stevie Wonder and Michael Jackson…"

"I like them, too." Chase flashed his teeth. "But I would've thought you would be more into Beyoncé, Alicia Keys, Seal or other similar artists."

"Oh, I think they're cool, too," Paula admitted.

"So you have a broad range of musical tastes?"

"Yes, you could say that, including a little jazz and classical music."

"Interesting." He hummed. "Maybe someday we can check out a concert."

Paula liked that idea. "Maybe we could," she said coyly.

Ten minutes later, Chase walked Paula out to her car. There was a bit of a chill in the early November air, and she would have welcomed being warmed by his strong arms. Or was that asking too much at this point?

"Thanks for putting together what looks to be a great concept," Chase told her.

"I had fun with it," she confessed. "Of course, we'd better wait till everything's in place for the final judgment."

He nodded. "I look forward to seeing the finished product."

Paula quivered. She wasn't sure if it was from being outside or from the images dancing in her head of sharing some romantic moments with him. Was he thinking the same thing?

Chase stepped closer. "I enjoyed our evening."

"Me, too." Paula saw no reason to deny it, and obviously he didn't, either.

"Perhaps we can do it again sometime—apart from business."

"I would like that," she said, happy he'd said he wanted to spend more time with her.

He licked his lips. "I was hoping you'd say that."

Paula could feel Chase's warm breath on her cheeks. She longed to feel his lips on hers.

Seemingly reading her thoughts, Chase tilted his head ever so slightly and gave Paula a soft, succulent kiss. It was more than enough for Paula to follow his lead. She stood on tiptoes and brought their lips together again, kissing him generously. She took in the woodsy scent of his cologne, which made him all the more appealing.

Chase put his arms around Paula's waist. She closed her eyes and saw stars. The kiss had left her breathless. Though Paula had never been too comfortable with public displays of affection, she felt she would kiss Chase McCord anywhere.

Paula drew back from Chase, feeling the sting of his lips on hers. "That was nice, but I think we'd better leave it there for now."

"All right." Chase's eyes twinkled with contentment. "And, yes, it was quite nice."

She suddenly felt warmed to the bone. "I'll call you to set up a time for the work to begin on your master suite," she said.

"I look forward to hearing from you." She unlocked the car with her remote and he opened the door for her. "Have a safe drive."

"I will," she promised. "See you soon."

"Bye for now."

Paula thought. She appreciated his thoughtfulness in opening the door for her. It was not something she was used to with men, but she welcomed it nonetheless. In fact, Chase was more of an all-around man than she had encountered in some time, if ever. She smiled to herself. The kiss had left Paula reeling with desire. It was definitely something to build on.

"He kissed me," Paula told her grandmother that evening.

Isabelle was sitting on a recliner. "Oh, really?"

"Well, actually we kissed each other." Paula couldn't help but confide in the one person with whom she had always been able to share the best and worst of her relationships. Not that dinner and a kiss constituted a relationship, but it still ranked in the "best" category in both respects.

"A good start," Isabelle stated with a nice smile on her face. "If the young man is anything like you've described, then I'd say he could be a real find for you."

Paula hated to burst her bubble yet didn't want to give Isa the wrong idea, either. "It's still way too soon to know just how real of a find he is. Or if anything meaningful will come out of this."

Isabelle took her reading glasses off. "No reason to look at the glass as half-empty, child," she insisted. "Maybe Chase won't wind up as the man of your dreams. Only the good Lord knows for sure. But if it's meant to happen, Chase could very well be the one who can put that sparkling diamond ring on your finger like the one I've got."

"Whoa…" Paula's mouth opened even as she noted Isa admiring her ring. "No one's talking about becoming engaged, much less getting married anytime soon."

Paula would love to walk down the aisle when the time was

right with a man who was just as willing. Whether Chase fell into that category was unclear at this point. Even if the man was totally past losing his wife, it didn't mean he had any desire to go beyond dating a woman in the foreseeable future.

Isabelle wrung her hands. "Nothing says one can't dream. That's what grandmothers do where it concerns their grandchildren. Besides, you're both young, successful, single people with your whole lives ahead of you. Since you're obviously attracted to each other, there's no reason why it can't potentially blossom into marriage. Maybe sooner than you might ever have imagined."

Paula laughed. "I think we still need to have our first official date before we elope."

"There will be no such thing," Isabelle said seriously. "When the time comes, and you're ready to say I do, it had better be a proper wedding. If I couldn't walk my daughter down the aisle, I most surely want to do it for my granddaughter."

It saddened Paula to think that her mother and Isa never had the type of relationship they deserved. The same was true where it concerned Paula and her mother. She would never want to deprive her grandmother of witnessing her marriage, which Paula hoped would happen while Isa was still alive.

Paula got up from the couch and hugged her. "I promise when that day comes, it won't be an elopement. I want all the trimmings of a big wedding, with my favorite grandmother sharing in every bit of the joy."

"Thank you for that." Tears welled in Isabelle's eyes. "I only want you to be happy."

Paula beamed at her grandmother. "You make me happy."

"A good man can make you happier." Isabelle took a breath. "Maybe you should invite Chase over so I can get to know him."

"*I* need to get to know him first," cautioned Paula. "It's important to me that we take our time to get comfortable with each other. Then I'll let you meet him."

Isabelle's eyes twinkled. "Fair enough. I don't want you to rush into anything. Heaven knows how that can backfire."

Paula bit her lip, thinking about putting nearly everything she had into her past relationships only to see them fall flat. If it was her destiny to be with Chase, she wouldn't force the issue. Something told her he was of the same mind. Paula thought about the sexual chemistry between them that had deepened when they kissed. She doubted any amount of reason could slow down the inevitable and spontaneous passions they seemed headed toward like a pair of runaway freight trains.

"It was just a kiss," Chase said, standing over the pool table in his father's recreation room. In truth, he saw it as much more. Paula was a good kisser, and he believed she was just as into their lips smooching as he was.

"Uh-huh." Sylvester studied his son. "Remember, you're talking to your father."

Chase grinned, deciding he might as well come clean. "All right, so it did mean something. I'm just not sure what it meant yet."

"I can fill in the blank," his father said astutely. "It means you're finally becoming human again instead of going through the motions as a man caught up in what was."

Chase put his cue stick on the table and sized up his next shot. "It hasn't been easy being on my own," he said truthfully.

"I know it hasn't. That's why I'm glad to see you are moving beyond a few dates with women who do little for you, other than provide eye candy, and taking concrete steps toward having a true lady in your life again." Sylvester rubbed his nose. "Especially this particular lady."

Chase called the shot, watching the ball hit a wall and roll into the pocket. "So what's up with you and Paula?" he asked suspiciously, as though the two were conspiring behind his back. "Is there something that I should know about?"

Sylvester shot quickly then chuckled. "Only that I have a fine eye for the lady I think would be great with my son. Never mind the fact she's also a damned good interior decorator with her own business."

"Did you ever tell Paula anything about me?" Chase asked curiously, wondering if she'd had an edge in seemingly hitting all the right marks to capture his attention.

Sylvester's right brow rose. "Such as?"

"That I'm a wealthy and lonely widower?"

"I didn't tell her anything, other than you were looking for an interior decorator." Sylvester ran his hand over his mouth. "If you're wondering if she might be after your money, think again. From what I know, she's got a thriving business. One of our biggest customers recommended her to redo this very room. That's why I gave you the scoop. It was totally up to you to contact her, which you did. As for the lonely part, you don't have a monopoly on that, son. Are you having second thoughts about Paula all of a sudden?"

"No," Chase said, feeling more secure about the relationship he and Paula were building. "Not really."

"Then what's the problem?"

Chase shrugged. "I guess I just hoped to get some added insight into her before things start to get serious."

Sylvester held up a beer bottle and chuckled. "That must have been some kiss."

"It was great," Chase admitted, recalling the moment. "More than that, I feel like I can relate to Paula beyond her physical appeal." He paused. "I just want to be sure we're compatible in all areas like…"

"Don't overthink this, Chase," Sylvester implored. "She's not Rochelle and never will be, but it doesn't mean that Paula doesn't offer just as much as a woman. Why don't you just enjoy her company?"

"Yeah, you're right." There was no need for him to get too carried away about everything being perfect between them when they hadn't even had their first real date yet. It was something Chase very much looked forward to in taking things to another plateau. "I won't go overboard in looking at the future and the past. I think I'll just work on the present right now and see how things turn out."

Sylvester grinned. "I'm glad you see it that way. I really hope the two of you find you're on to something great here. You're way too young to be moping around all by yourself. Trust me when I tell you there will be better times ahead in your personal life."

Chase smiled, warmed by the thought. "Hope so." He remained cautious but optimistic that Paula was someone with whom he might be able to make a serious connection. He couldn't deny that she was a great kisser, which only made him hungry to see if she was just as great in bed.

"Are you ever going to take that shot, or what?" Sylvester asked wryly. "I'm not getting any younger standing here waiting."

Chase chuckled and aimed the cue stick. "Eight ball in the corner pocket," he said before declaring victory.

Chapter 7

On Saturday afternoon, Paula supervised the work while her contractor's crew moved things in and out of Chase's master suite. Since she was ultimately responsible for any mishap or damage, she urged everyone to be careful as always. In this case, Paula was especially conscious of the beautiful surroundings. Wanting to continue to make a good impression on Chase, she sought to finish the project as quickly as possible and get a solid thumbs-up from him.

"Where do you want this?" asked Jim, a crew member, as he and another man brought in the entertainment cabinet.

"Let's put it right along this wall," Paula directed. She watched with satisfaction when it fit perfectly.

Jackie, the housekeeper, came in as they went out. "What can I do to help?"

"Well, as soon as everything's in place, you can help me put the new sheets and covers on the bed," Paula told her.

"Will do. Just give me a shout when you're ready."

"Thanks, Jackie."

Paula imagined it must be nice to have someone to keep the place tidy for a busy man like Chase with his wife no longer there to do her part. While Isa did many of the chores at home, mostly out of boredom and with too much time on her hands, Paula was only too happy to pitch in. The same would be true were she living with a man. Paula had no problem holding up her end in maintaining a clean, comfortable household. She thought about Chase. She had asked him to stay away for a couple of hours so he wouldn't be tempted to check out the progress before the work was complete.

Paula walked over to one of the windows, where Bradford was installing the cellular shades. "How's it going up there?" she asked.

"Just about through," Bradford said with a sigh.

"Good."

"I'll get Chad started on the other one and make sure nothing's been left undone."

Paula nodded. "So far everything seems to be going along smoothly."

"You think he's gonna want us to give the whole house a makeover?" Bradford asked hopefully.

"One never knows," Paula said with a smile, confident she could do wonderful things with any room in the house. She wouldn't press her luck, though. The fact was, Chase couldn't go wrong with the rooms as they were. For that, Paula gave kudos to his late wife for her incredible vision and sense of space.

Paula understood that Chase was simply interested in starting over again, in his residence and personal life. She was glad Chase had let her into his life on both counts. She welcomed the opportunity to be an interior decorator and a woman to him, knowing she was getting a good man with many qualities in return.

Chase drove around town after spending the morning at work, busying himself with multiple tasks that were required as president of the company. With the economy struggling right now, the diamond business was not as bustling as in other years. But it was still pretty good compared to other types of businesses. A number of new jewelry stores had popped up in the area recently as competition—testimony that selling diamonds and other gems was a resilient business. It was one Chase embraced wholeheartedly in following his father's lead.

His thoughts turned to Paula. He was dying to get home and see if her vision measured up when all was said and done. Though a small part of him was saddened at the thought of undoing Rochelle's magnificent decorative efforts, the better part of Chase believed it was long overdue in his bedroom. He had to escape the feeling of sorrow every time he set foot in there. This was an opportunity to do just that and, at the same time, start thinking of the room again as a place for peaceful sleep and possibly making an intimate connection.

He dropped by a store and picked up something for dinner. His cell phone rang while he was in the parking lot. It was Paula. Chase found himself smiling as a result. "Hope you're calling to tell me I can come home and check out your handiwork."

"That's exactly why I'm calling," she said energetically. "We're all done."

"How does it look?" he asked impatiently.

"You'll have to decide that for yourself."

Chase sighed. "Well, I'm just around the corner, so I'll see you shortly."

"Bye," Paula said.

Chase disconnected and smiled thoughtfully. He liked the sound of Paula's sexy voice. What she would sound like in bed while he pleasured her? The notion turned him on in a way he hadn't felt in quite some time. He checked the feeling, deciding it was best right now to focus on the lady as an interior decorator in his employ. She had given another room in his house a makeover, and the least he could do was respect that side of her.

Paula felt jittery as Chase took his time looking around the master suite. She was pretty certain it would meet with his approval, but until the words came out of his mouth, there was always the possibility that he could find something he didn't like. If so, she would fix it, wanting complete satisfaction for her clients. This was particularly important with Chase, whom Paula was starting to see as much more than just another employer.

"You never fail to amaze me," Chase said, looking Paula right in the eye. "I feel like I'm stepping into this room for the first time. It's incredible!"

You're incredible, she thought, admiring him in his double-breasted charcoal suit.

Paula blushed. "I'm so glad you're okay with it."

"That goes for all of us." Bradford spoke on behalf of the crew.

Chase grinned. "I really appreciate the transformation."

Bradford put his hand on Chase's shoulder. "Hey, you paid for the job, and Paula stayed on our butts to make sure we delivered."

"You certainly did deliver," Chase said flatly. "I definitely got my money's worth."

"In that case, our work is done." Bradford looked at Paula. "When you need my services again, you know how to reach me."

"I'll definitely be in touch," she promised, knowing there were already a couple of jobs in the works.

Paula saw the crew out the door. When she came back, her thoughts were squarely on Chase and where he wanted to go from there, both professionally and personally. She found him in the great room with Jackie.

"Can you come in an extra day next week?" Chase asked Jackie. "I've got some things in a storage room I'd like to clear out and donate."

"Any day in particular?"

"Whatever day works best for you," Chase said.

Jackie pondered it. "I can swing by on Thursday afternoon."

Chase nodded. "That's fine."

Jackie faced Paula. "I love what you did to the bedroom."

"Thanks," Paula voiced. "I enjoyed redecorating it."

"Maybe I can get you to take a look at my apartment sometime," Jackie said. "I can't afford too much, but you could probably give me some good pointers."

Paula smiled. "I'd be happy to." She glanced at Chase, who hadn't taken his eyes off her since she came into the room. "Or if you want to hire me, I'm sure we could work something out."

Jackie grinned. "Cool."

"Just be sure to send her back when you're through," Chase said jokingly. "I might need more of Ms. Devine's services myself."

"There's enough of me to go around," Paula offered with amusement, glad to know her talents were so appreciated.

"I wouldn't doubt that for a moment." Chase gave a chuckle.

"I'll see you next week," Jackie told him.

Paula handed her a card. "Give me a call."

"I will," she promised.

After Jackie left, Chase walked up to Paula. "Thanks for making yourself available to her."

"Interior decoration is what I do. I'm happy to help anyone I can to improve the appearance and functionality of their living space."

"I can see that." His eyes angled at hers. "What other rooms in my house do you feel could use some improvement?"

She fluttered her lashes. "Seriously?"

"Yes. I'm open to hearing your ideas, since you've done such a marvelous job so far."

Paula knew this was a tremendous opportunity to continue to modernize his beautiful home. She could think of a couple of rooms that would benefit from her expertise. However, she wasn't sure if it was a good idea to keep working for someone she was becoming far more interested in on a personal level. Or maybe that was the whole point of his proposition, to maintain their ties so they could explore any romantic potential.

"I'll need to look around more to get a better idea of what I would recommend to enhance what you already have," she told him.

"Well, feel free to look around as much as you like," Chase offered.

Paula sighed. "You are more than generous."

"I can afford to be, especially if I sense that I can get a good return on my investment."

"And what exactly are you investing in?" Paula asked with more than a little curiosity.

He held her gaze. "How about a lady who appeals to me on multiple levels?"

Paula warmed. "That sounds tempting."

"I've also never been more serious," Chase said, continuing to look at her. "I think you're lovely, sexy, smart and obviously very talented."

"Don't stop now." She felt a wave of anticipation for what might come next.

"I won't."

Chase cupped her cheeks and, angling his head perfectly, kissed Paula tenderly on the lips. She felt his lower lip in her mouth and sucked it, enjoying his taste and wanting more. Opening her mouth, she took in all of his, sticking her tongue inside. He reciprocated, and their tongues danced while the kiss deepened. Chase wrapped his arms around her lower back, drawing them even closer without breaking their liplock or the sexual tension in the air.

Paula swallowed and felt light on her feet. The kiss was hot and heavy, igniting passions that had been building between them like a wildfire. Her breasts pressed against Chase's hard chest, stimulating Paula's nipples. She wanted to scream with joy, but instead concentrated on the potency of a kiss that was draining all her energy and putting it squarely into the man who was doing this to her. She could feel Chase's erection throbbing against her leg.

He wants me as much as I do him.

The thought left Paula even hungrier. She opened her mouth wider and flattened Chase's lips desperately with the lingering kiss. He gave as much in return, tilting his face in the opposite direction and sucking her tongue while rolling his hands across her back. Paula grew hot with desire as the kiss rose to a new level. She cradled Chase's head in her hands, making him her prisoner while their lips conquered one another's, seeking out every ounce of pleasure they could.

This is crazy, thought Paula, her heart racing wildly. Never before had a kiss turned her on like this. Chase knew what he was doing and did it very well. It almost made her feel as if there had never been anyone before her to benefit from the powerful persuasion of his mesmerizing kisses. This was more than enough for Paula to want to delve much further into the mutual exploration that gripped her from head to toe. She continued to take full command of Chase's mouth and give him all he could handle of hers.

They moved around in a slow, seductive circle, never allowing any air to come between their ravenous mouths till Paula could no longer differentiate between her lips and his. She caught her breath, eager to explore the wonders of this man thoroughly. She was exhilarated by the kiss and dizzy with want that only Chase could satisfy.

Chase was so wrapped up in the kiss that he lost all sense of time and place. Paula's mouth was deliciously sweet, full and sensuous, her face smooth to the touch. His hands roamed freely while their mouths sucked greedily. Kissing Paula had aroused Chase to a point where he could barely hold back his desire to make love to her. He cupped her buttocks through the fabric of her skirt and felt Paula wince. His chest heaved as it rubbed against Paula's hardened nipples beneath her blouse. He was intoxicated by her taste, as well as her flowery perfume.

I can't wait any longer to be inside her.

Chase unlocked their lips and saw that Paula's were swollen from the kiss. Her lower lip quivered slightly. He looked into her eyes and they stared back at him lasciviously. "I want you," he said huskily.

"Then take me," she demanded. "And I'll take you."

"Wait right here."

Chase left her in the great room and dashed to the bathroom down the hall. He opened the drawer and took out a box of condoms, removing one. The need to be inside Paula was almost overpowering. Clearly she shared his feelings. Now they would make it happen.

Back in her presence, their mouths engaged again hotly before Chase started removing Paula's clothing and helping her to strip him of his. His heart pounded at the thought of seeing her naked. After they were both unclothed, he took a moment to marvel at the exquisiteness of Paula's body. Shapely and sexy, she had full, high breasts that were perfectly rounded and a narrow waist expanding gently into firm hips. Her legs were lean and long, her toenails perfectly manicured on lovely feet.

"You're so beautiful," he told her enthrallingly.

Paula's lips opened slightly, but she said nothing. The lustful look dancing in her eyes told Chase all he needed to know. Her fingers ran nimbly across his chest, then along Chase's jawline. He salivated at the vision of making love to this incredible woman right now. Taking her hand, he began to suck each finger one by one. They were soft and sweet; a prelude to what awaited him with the rest of her body.

Chase brought Paula to the sectional, where she lay down and splayed her legs invitingly. He quickly tore open the condom from his pants pocket and slid it onto his erection that threatened to explode at any moment, so great was his pent-up desire. Leaning down, Chase kissed Paula's lips passionately as he put his hand between her legs. She was very wet, letting him know that she was as ready as he was to make love.

He entered her, and she immediately clamped around him, drawing him farther inside. Unable to control himself, Chase thrust deeper and harder. Paula moaned loudly while probing his mouth with her lips and tongue. Grasping one of her breasts, Chase gently rubbed the nipple with his thumb until it hardened. She ran her long nails roughly across his back while they slammed their bodies against one another frenetically before yielding to the power of primordial desire.

Chase gripped Paula's buttocks as he felt his surge coming. He drove deep into her and stayed there while his orgasm took hold of him powerfully. Simultaneously, Paula's contractions came in waves around his penis as she climaxed. They were both panting and kissing wildly while they reached the heights of first-time sexual ecstasy before the feelings subsided, leaving them sweaty, spent and breathless.

"You were incredible," Chase told Paula, kissing her soft shoulder.

"So were you." She had her leg draped across his. The scent of sex resonated in the air, appealing to her sense of smell like never before.

"I'm sorry if it all happened way too fast," Chase apologized.

The truth was, she was so turned on by him that Paula had also wanted it fast and furious, with a potent conclusion. "It's all right," she said, her face upturned. "I doubt either of us could've waited any longer."

He kissed her shoulder again. "I think you're right."

She smiled. There would be other times to take it nice and slow.

Chase kissed her left breast. "Let me make it up to you."

Paula's nipple tingled at the touch of his lips. "What did you have in mind?"

"Why don't we pick up where we left off upstairs?"

She hoisted a brow. "Your bedroom?"

"Yeah."

"Are you sure?" Paula didn't want Chase to feel uncomfortable being with her in the room he'd shared with his late wife.

Chase met her eyes. "What better way to break in the newly refurbished room?" He ran his hand down the side of Paula's face. "I'm okay with putting the past behind me and working on the present—and beyond…."

Paula sighed and kissed his hand. "So am I."

"Then we're definitely in sync," he said.

She licked her lips. "Yes, I'd say we definitely are."

He grinned seductively. "I like the sound of that."

Chase kissed her, teasing her tongue with his. Paula felt herself growing aroused again and wanted to experience passion between them that was prolonged and even more satisfying. She continued the kiss, loving the feel of his lips upon hers. The sensations they emitted radiated throughout her body. Had she ever gotten so worked up from a man's kiss before? The answer was clear, as Paula found herself totally into Chase and wanting to bring their sexuality to new heights. He broke away and stood, reaching for her hand. She read the carnal hunger in his eyes, matching hers.

Chapter 8

They were still holding hands and naked when Paula walked Chase into the room. Instead of seeing the bedroom as a showcase of her decorating skills, she was fixated on the man. Chase was the most perfect man Paula had ever seen up close and in person. He had an unblemished coat of sleek brown skin exposed over a lean, mean body. A broad chest narrowed into rock-hard abs, with taut thighs and the solid, long legs of an African-American Adonis. His buttocks were rounded and firm. The enormity and splendor of his erection sent a rush of desire through Paula.

Looking up at his square jaw, she rested her eyes on the wide contours of Chase's mouth, imagining it leaving searing kisses all over her body. She followed the lines that blended his facial hair and turned to a broad nose with a small bridge. Her survey of the man ended when Paula looked beneath thick, dark brows into the depths of coal eyes that were engaged upon her voraciously.

"I want you again in the worst way," she murmured, unabashed.

"I'm lusting for you just as badly," Chase said.

Paula sank onto the bed and slid atop the covers. She waited anxiously as Chase slipped on another condom. When he joined her, they embraced and resumed the passionate kissing that sent Paula into a tizzy. She ran her hands all over Chase, and he reciprocated, tickling and stimulating her.

Chase's mouth left Paula's lips and moved to her neck, where he kissed and licked her with measured precision. She loved how he made her feel. His hot kisses moved down to her breasts, where he ran his tongue repeatedly across one nipple, then the other. Paula gasped from the sheer pleasure radiating from her hardened nipples.

Chase trailed down Paula's stomach with his tongue, delighting her. She watched with enchantment as he buried his face between her legs. She flinched when he began to kiss her clitoris. He nibbled gently around the outer edges then licked and sucked relentlessly.

"You taste so good," he told her greedily before spreading Paula's thighs farther and continuing his onslaught.

Paula squeezed her eyes shut and trembled violently as her body responded to his erotic attention. She felt all control go out the window, as she was about to come at any moment now and couldn't hold back.

"Oh, Chase," she murmured. "Mmm…"

She bit her lip, moving her head from side to side as the sensations built. As the waves of ecstasy began to overpower her, Paula brazenly held Chase's head in place while he orally gratified her. A strangled cry escaped Paula's lips when she came in blissful surrender. Chase clutched her legs firmly as she threatened to elevate off the bed from the powerful climax. Only after the sensations started to subside did Paula shamelessly release his head from her grasp.

Chase lifted his head up, his yearning for her evident in his intense expression. She wanted him just as much, longing to feel him inside her. Paula watched as Chase's erect penis plunged inside her body. She took him in, constricting around his penis and drawing him in deeper.

Chase lay down on Paula, and she wrapped her legs high around his back, absorbing his powerful thrusts while arching her back to increase her pleasure. Their mouths were pressed together tightly, sucking each other's lips with a sense of urgency as the fire within them built. They made love with passion and purpose, panting and perspiring in their determined effort to gratify one another like nothing else mattered.

Paula found herself growing exhausted as she matched Chase's intensity step for step, inch for inch, breath for breath. But she wouldn't have it any other way, as their physical chemistry and sexual urges demanded such mutual gratification. At some point, she ended up on top of him, cradling Chase's hard body between her thighs. Paula ran her fingers across his nipples as his erection stimulated her. She brought him deep inside her vagina and then lifted to the shaft of his penis torturously, squeezing to enhance his pleasure, before he once again burrowed to the depths within.

Chase grunted loudly, and Paula moaned harmonically as they kept up their frenetic pace. Paula's body quivered and her breaths quickened as her orgasm reverberated throughout her body. Soon after, Chase shuddered as he reached the apex of his climax. He wrapped Paula tightly in his arms while they rode the wave of sexual delight together.

When Paula awakened, she was still in Chase's sturdy arms. She felt especially sexy and wanted. Moreover, she was in the company of a man she really liked. She was amazed how compatible they were in bed, almost as though they had been lovers for years. How was that possible?

With her previous lovers, it had taken time to get used to each other's likes and dislikes, along with style and substance. But everything had flowed so naturally with Chase, like he could read her mind and she, in turn, knew exactly what he was thinking beforehand. Paula was pleased, but not sure what to make of this.

Paula looked at his face in the fading light. He was asleep and snoring lightly. She moved slowly out of his grasp. Sliding down the bed, Paula grabbed Chase's flaccid penis. She licked the tip, which caused Chase to stir a little. Paula licked him again and watched with pleasure as he started to become erect. Having a strong desire to be fulfilled by Chase once again, Paula put her mouth over his penis and ran her tongue across the top. She brought him to the base of her throat, ignoring the tickling sensation as her mouth engulfed him.

Chase woke up and began to stroke her hair. Paula slowly moved her mouth up and down his penis, feeling his body tremble with her movement. She held his legs down while she brought Chase to a rousing climax. She wanted to give him this release, to please him as he had pleased her.

Afterward, Paula lifted up, meeting Chase's sleepy gaze. "I hope you didn't mind my waking you?"

"Not at all."

She smiled teasingly. "I didn't think so."

"You are remarkable," Chase told her blithely.

"So are you," she returned dreamily.

Paula wished they could carry on a bit more and explore some new territory, but she had to restrain herself for now. She extricated herself from under the covers and climbed off the bed.

"Are you coming back?" Chase asked, stretching his long limbs out. "Or shall we go another round?"

"It's getting late," Paula said. "I should probably be going." Though she would love to stay the night, she didn't want to wear out her welcome. Or get too comfortable till they had spent more time together outside of bed.

"I understand." A look of disappointment crossed Chase's face. "So, when can I see you again?"

"How does tomorrow sound?" she asked, batting her lashes.

Chase grinned approvingly. "Sounds perfect."

Paula was aware that Chase was checking out her nude body. It surprised her that she felt totally at ease with him at this early stage of their relationship. Perhaps it was because they had become so familiar with each other in the space of a few hours that there was hardly anything left to the imagination. Yet Paula's mind was full of wild fantasies she hoped they would be able to explore together.

Paula couldn't stop thinking about Chase during the drive home. They had gone from client and decorator to lovers so quickly. She could scarcely believe that he was the same man she had met at the coffee shop. She felt things had certainly changed for the better since that day. Given her track record, she wouldn't begin to predict how things might end up between them. Better to just take things slowly and hope what happened today was merely a prelude of what tomorrow could bring.

When Paula got home, she found her grandmother lying on the couch in the living room. Isabelle appeared to be asleep, with her reading glasses precariously resting on her nose and an open book on her lap. It wasn't unusual for her to be asleep on the couch, but as Isa got older, Paula often feared she might be dead.

Her heart lurched. "Isa…"

Isabelle's eyes fluttered open groggily. "Oh, you're home."

"Yes." Paula sighed. "I was worried about you."

Isabelle sat up. "You needn't have been, child. I'm not about to die anytime soon, and certainly not before it's my time to go. I guess I must have dozed off just when I was getting into the meat of this novel."

Paula was relieved. She hoped her grandmother would live to be one hundred, maybe even longer. And Paula planned to follow suit, especially if there was someone loving to grow old with.

"You're home kind of late," Isabelle noted, pushing her glasses back up.

Paula flinched. "I know, and I'm sorry. I should've called."

Isabelle waved her off. "You're a grown woman. You don't have to explain yourself to me."

Paula sat down next to her, feeling compelled to say something anyway. "I was with Chase."

"I gathered as much." Isabelle looked at her fondly. "I take it he liked the redecorating?"

"Yes, he was quite pleased with the work."

"But even more pleased with you?" Isabelle suggested.

Paula chuckled, knowing there was little her grandmother couldn't figure out.

"That, too," she admitted. "I'd have to say I was just as pleased with him."

Isabelle's eyes crinkled. "I'm happy to hear that, though not surprised. The way you've spoken of Chase tells me that you're definitely interested in the young man. It's good to know that it goes both ways."

"I think it does," Paula said confidently.

"Who knows what the future has in store for you two?" Isabelle said hopefully.

"We're just getting started in our relationship," Paula reminded her, "so don't go getting any wild ideas."

Isabelle laughed. "I wouldn't dream of it. Besides, I'll leave that part to you." She paused. "Are you hungry?"

"Not really." Paula's appetite had been squelched by a different kind of nourishment.

"Well, come and have a cup of tea with me anyway. Then we can both head off to bed," her grandmother said.

"Uh, okay…" Paula sensed there was something else on Isabelle's mind and expected to hear all about it.

"You had a visitor this evening," Isabelle said mysteriously as they sat in the breakfast nook.

"Who was it?" Paula couldn't even begin to hazard a guess.

"Your ex-beau."

Paula's eyes widened. "Sheldon?"

"Yes, I believe he was your last boyfriend," Isabelle said as she stirred honey into her tea.

"Don't remind me." Paula stiffened at the thought. "What did he want?"

"To see you," Isabelle said with a catch to her voice. "Obviously, the man doesn't know when to leave well enough alone."

Obviously. "What did you tell him?"

"That you weren't home, and he shouldn't bother coming back."

Paula smiled at her grandmother's outspoken nature, which she'd passed down the line. "Think he got the message?"

Isabelle rolled her eyes. "One can only hope. No telling with that one."

"Maybe I should talk to him," Paula said tonelessly.

Isabelle frowned. "What on earth for?"

"You know that it ended kind of awkwardly between us, but ended nevertheless," she made clear.

"Right, and sometimes that happens when one person wants out and the other doesn't," her grandmother said bluntly. "He wasn't right for you, and you did the correct thing by breaking it off. If Sheldon was offended, he'll just have to deal with it."

Paula could not have agreed more. But she also knew how some men were, trying to hold on to something no longer there, in spite of themselves.

"And what if he doesn't go away easily?"

"He doesn't have any choice," Isabelle pointed out. "You've moved on."

"You're right," Paula said, determined not to allow him to get to her. "What's done is done."

"So I say leave it alone and focus on your relationship with Chase. It's one that clearly has much more promise."

Paula's lashes fluttered. "How can you be so sure? Maybe I'm just doomed to end up in one dead-end relationship after another."

"Nonsense," Isabelle insisted with a dismissive wave of her hand. "You don't believe that any more than I do."

"I just want to be happy with someone," Paula said.

"You can be. In fact, I'd say that someone just may be in the picture right now."

Paula sipped her tea contemplatively. "I hope so."

She regretted her relationship with Sheldon, knowing she had used poor judgment in going out with him. She didn't want to experience that again. But Chase was a different type of person altogether, and Paula believed that what they had established in a short time seemed more real than any of her other relationships had. She was optimistic that they really were starting something potentially very special.

Chapter 9

Chase stared out the window of his office at McCord Diamonds, daydreaming about last night. Making love to Paula had proven to be everything he'd expected and so much more. She had done wonders to make him feel like a man again. Somehow Paula had managed to tap into his psyche and make him see things in a new light. Chase believed he had met someone with whom he could really relate. That was certainly true in bed, where they seemed as compatible as he could ever have imagined.

But their connection ran much deeper than that. Paula was her own woman and independently successful like him. She wasn't after him for money or status. They just seemed to hit it off, and he was very interested in seeing if things would continue to blossom between them.

Chase snapped out of his reverie when he saw Monica standing in the doorway.

"Busy?" she asked, holding a folder in her hand.

"I'm never too busy for my best friend." He smiled. "What's up?"

"We need to review the international collections."

Chase nodded. "Okay. Have a seat."

Monica sat in a leather chair across from his desk. "We have new gemstone designs from Hong Kong and Thailand." She handed him information to that effect. "I'm particularly excited about the new diamond necklaces and pendants."

Chase studied the photographs before him. "I can see why." He envisioned putting one around Paula's neck. "What else do we have?"

"Our three-and-a-half carat, four- to six-prong set diamond wedding rings," Monica said, passing him the data. "A perfect way to say 'I love you' to any lady."

He smiled. "I couldn't agree more."

Chase admired the pictures of three-stone rings in twenty-four-carat gold or platinum. He wondered if he would get another chance to put a diamond ring on a woman's finger. He had previously felt the notion of marriage had died with Rochelle, but now he could envision walking down the aisle again someday.

"We have new half-carat diamond bracelets in white or yellow gold," Monica said, "and some remarkable loose diamonds."

Chase reviewed the photographs and descriptions, homing in on a nearly colorless heart-shaped diamond. "Very nice," he said evenly.

"Wait till you see our new line of chocolate-diamond rings with black rhodium," Monica told him excitedly. "They're absolutely gorgeous!"

"I'm sure they are," Chase said abstractedly.

"Not exactly edible, but these chocolate babies certainly would wet many a woman's appetite."

Monica laughed, but Chase barely heard it. His mind had drifted off into thinking about Paula and how much she had come to mean to him in such a short time. He saw her as potential marriage material, though he was uncertain if she viewed things the same way. Maybe they were only comforting each other for the short run, till the real thing came along. Or maybe their compatibility, sexual and otherwise, had proven itself, and the future prospects were brighter than ever.

He eyed Monica as she continued talking about the wonders of chocolate diamonds before interrupting her. "Do you want to grab a bite to eat?"

"Sure, why not." Monica glanced at her watch. "It is lunchtime."

Chase gave her a tiny grin and headed for the door.

"I met someone," he told Monica as they sat in a delicatessen.

"Is that so?" She met his gaze.

"Her name is Paula. She did the redecorating at my house."

"Hmm, that's interesting." Monica studied him. "So, how long has this been going on?"

Chase lifted his roast beef sandwich. "Not too long." Though it seemed as if they had known each other for some time.

"I'm glad to see you haven't let a few bad dates since Rochelle's death ruin your outlook altogether," Monica told him.

Chase swallowed. "Couldn't do that. I figured it was only a matter of time before I clicked with someone."

"You know Rochelle is up there rooting you on, don't you?"

"Yeah, I do," he said thoughtfully.

"When she died, she didn't want to take your heart with her. You have a right to meet someone who can make you every bit as happy as she did."

"I was thinking the same thing." Chase wiped his mouth. "I feel pretty happy when I'm with Paula."

Monica bit into a ranch fry. "And she feels the same way about you?"

"I think so. We're just getting started in the dating game. So far, so good."

"I see." Monica looked at him squarely. "When do I get to meet her?"

Chase expected no less from his friend. "I was hoping we could get together next week."

She nodded. "Count me in."

He smiled. "Consider yourself counted."

"I promise I won't be too judgmental."

Chase chuckled. "Since when?"

Monica grinned. "You know you wouldn't have it any other way."

"True. We've always had each other's back."

"That's what sincere friendship is all about," she said.

"Agreed." Chase dipped a ranch fry in ketchup while musing about his new romantic friendship with Paula. "I'll set it up."

"If you don't mind, I'd like to bring along a date," Monica said, lifting her corned beef sandwich.

"Of course." Chase regarded her curiously. "Who's the lucky guy?"

She hesitated. "You remember Zachary, the gemologist?"

His right brow lifted. "The same one you had a problem with?"

"Oh, we're past that now," Monica said with a chuckle.

"Is that so?" Chase teased her.

"What can I say? The man's a hunk and has more energy than he knows what to do with. Fortunately that's not an issue with me, since I know exactly how to harness it."

Chase laughed. "Spare me the details." He certainly was in no hurry to delve too deeply into the details of his sexual relationship with Paula. As far as he was concerned, that was something private between them. He was hopeful they could replay the theme over and over.

"Do we all assemble at your place?" asked Monica, sipping root beer. "Or at a restaurant?"

Chase leaned back. "My house. That way you and Zach can check out Paula's work."

"Cool. I can't wait to meet her. I'm sure she's all that and more if she caught your eye."

"The lady is very attractive," he admitted, "and quite talented, too."

"And I suppose her personality is sparkling, as well?"

Chase chuckled. "Like champagne on ice."

Monica gave him a playful frown. "I'm jealous already."

"You two have the same qualities," Chase said. "True gems. And I'll bet Zachary's already discovered that."

She grinned. "Now I know why we've always been such good friends. You're a natural charmer. I'm sure you swept Paula right off her feet."

Chase grinned crookedly, while imagining Paula off her feet in bed. "Probably more the other way around," he said. "We'll see how it goes."

Paula sat in her office, literally counting the minutes till she saw Chase again this evening. The powerful effects of yesterday's lovemaking still had her reeling. She felt aroused contemplating an encore performance that could well exceed any expectations.

Paula's cell phone rang. She saw that the caller was Sheldon Burke. Her heart sank.

What does he want? As if I can't guess.

Paula chose not to answer it, not wanting to give him any encouragement that there was a chance of rekindling their relationship. What they had was strictly in the past, never to be repeated. Her focus now was on one man, a very incredible, ultrasexy man named Chase McCord.

A few hours later, Paula stood at Chase's doorstep, feeling anxious. He opened the door wearing a Seattle Seahawks jersey and form-fitting jeans.

"Hey," he said, grinning. "Come in."

Paula got a whiff of his cologne as she passed by him. The man always smelled good, which, along with his incredible masculinity, made him all the more appealing.

"Can I get you something to drink?" Chase asked.

She faced him, overcome with desire. "Why don't we go upstairs instead?" she voiced bravely.

Chase's eyes widened eargerly. "I like the sound of that."

"I thought you might." Paula turned her chin up and kissed him hungrily, enjoying the taste of his wondrous lips. She forced herself to pull back, hard as it was to stop kissing him.

Chase touched his lips. "Keep that up and we'll never make it to the bedroom."

"Don't tempt me," she warned. Paula could hardly keep her clothes on or stop herself from ripping his off.

Chase scooped her into his arms and mounted the stairs as their mouths once again connected and Paula fell hard under his spell. In the master suite, they stripped naked without ado as lovers sure of themselves. Paula pushed Chase onto the bed and pounced atop him, peppering his face with sweet kisses. She licked his nose, then his lips, before nibbling on his ears and chin. She found herself wanting to experience every inch of this man.

Paula's mouth conquered his zealously even as her hand made its way to Chase's penis. It was hard and throbbing, obviously ready for her. She stroked him and felt his fingers rubbing against her clitoris. This sent streaks of fire shooting throughout her body. She tried hard to contain herself, biting Chase's lip. His sure fingertips were not making it easy, deftly stroking her most private part like a master of erotic torture. She was close to coming.

In an instant, Chase had rolled on top of Paula and locked on to the raw need in her eyes. She made no attempt to shy away from her nearly overwhelming desire.

"Get inside me," she pleaded breathlessly.

His face grew intense. "Your wish is my command!"

He slipped into a condom and parted her thighs. She arched her back and lunged forward to meet his penis halfway, till it was wedged deep inside her. Paula absorbed Chase's persuasive thrusts, each one of which hit the target of her pleasure skillfully and vigorously. A prolonged moan of ecstatic surrender escaped Paula as she willingly gave herself to Chase and demanded he do the same in return. He pressed his hands into the bed, supporting himself while making love to her in a fluid and determined motion.

Paula's body was blazing with desire for him. She dug her nails into the flesh of Chase's buttocks and saw him wince. He licked and sucked her nipples relentlessly, giving her untold enjoyment.

"Kiss me," she murmured, eager to have his lips on hers as the buildup brought them total satisfaction.

"With all the pleasure in the world," Chase voiced hoarsely.

He lowered his mouth to her waiting lips, kissing her passionately. Paula's tongue circled the inside of his lips, tracing the moist softness and rolling across his teeth before twirling around Chase's tongue. He reciprocated with his tongue as ardor guided them in a powerful kiss that left Paula totally enraptured.

With their bodies locked in coitus and dripping with perspiration, Paula moved higher onto Chase's erection, bringing him deeper inside. She held on to his shoulder blades and quavered madly as his penis moved against her clitoris in the perfect blend of sexual stimulation.

"Chase… Oh, Chase," Paula sang gutturally and clutched him tightly while her orgasm flooded her body with numbing ecstasy. She shook uncontrollably and constricted around him demandingly.

Encouraged by this, Chase propelled himself into her with abandon. Sensing his orgasm coming, Paula helped him along by increasing her constrictions and moving her hips in unison with his. He came with a thunderous jolt, practically elevating the bed as their bodies moved harmoniously with passion and pleasure.

Minutes later, they lay there spent and satiated, their limbs still tangled.

"Wow!" Chase said, resting his hand on Paula's damp buttock.

She laughed. "That good, huh?"

"Much better than good. It was something totally out of this world."

"I have to agree with you," Paula admitted, breathing in the arousing scent of their terrific sex.

He kissed her breast. "I just can't seem to get enough of you."

Paula's lashes fluttered. "Excuse me, but I believe I was the one who seduced you."

"Good point." Chase wet his lips salaciously. "It looks like we just can't keep our hands off each other."

"You have a problem with that, mister?" she teased.

"Yeah, I do."

Paula met his eyes. "Oh?"

Chase grinned. "Now that you're in my system, it's almost impossible to focus on anything else."

"We could always cool things for a while if you want," she suggested, hoping he wasn't hinting at that.

"I don't think so," he said in no uncertain terms. "We're just getting started."

"I'm glad you feel that way," she said, relief in her voice.

His eyes twinkled. "There is no other way to feel. You've brought excitement back into my life. It's not something I take lightly."

Paula looked up at him. "So it's not just sexual?"

A look of sincerity crossed Chase's face. "Not to me. We're certainly amazing together in bed, but I believe there's more to this than sex."

She had no problem with Chase feeling that way, as the same thing had occurred to her. Paula felt a new surge of confidence in their relationship, but decided it was best to take a conservative approach for the time being, lest she get hurt.

"Maybe there is," she said coyly. "Let's just enjoy what we have and see how things progress."

Chase kissed the valley between her breasts. "That's fine by me. I don't think either of us will have much trouble enjoying each other over and over again."

"Neither do I."

Paula felt a tingling sensation where his lips had just parted, sensing they were about to go at it again. She was really starting to like Chase, but didn't want to get her hopes up that this might lead to something truly lasting, only to be deflated.

Chapter 10

Chase felt like a new man with Paula in his life. He hadn't understood the depth of the void left by Rochelle's death. Until Paula, he didn't know how happy he could be. Their sexual chemistry couldn't be better, and they were clearly making strides as friends.

They were standing in Chase's den. Paula looked sexy wearing one of his shirts and nothing else. She was assessing the room, which was the first one he and Rochelle had furnished when they moved here. In his mind, it seemed a bit outdated. Maybe Paula would disagree.

"I love the space in here," she said, looking around. "It doesn't seem like it gets much use."

"Not lately," Chase conceded. "I tend to spend most of my time here in my office, the great room or the master suite."

The thought of how they had spent the past hour or so in bed brought a licentious smile to his lips. Maybe they could pick up where the passion ended. He was certainly game, and he suspected it wouldn't take much persuasion to get Paula on board.

"I like the layout of the furniture," she told him, "but I think it could use some pizzazz, along with some new accent pieces and maybe a nice Persian rug."

"Go for it," Chase said agreeably, trying to stay focused on the subject at hand.

"Are you sure?" Paula brushed against him. "I don't want our involvement to cause you to lose objectivity when it comes to redecorating your house."

Chase appreciated her concern, given the personal and business relationship they had forged. He wrapped his arms around her waist. "My objectivity is just fine," he said firmly to set her mind at ease. "I'm hiring you for your interior-decoration talents, not your skills in the bedroom. That isn't to say I don't appreciate those skills every bit as much, if not more," he teased.

Paula's lashes batted flirtatiously. "You would say that while I'm standing here wearing nothing but your shirt."

Chase gave her the once-over and felt aroused. "It sure looks much nicer on you than it ever could on me."

"Oh, you think so, do you?"

"Would I lie?" he asked with amusement.

"You tell me," she challenged.

Chase took the bait. He angled his face and kissed her tasty lips. It was something he could do all day and night.

"I believe you," Paula said into his mouth, chuckling, before she slithered out of Chase's grasp. "I would be happy to give your den a makeover."

He grinned with satisfaction. "I'm sure you'll turn it into something I can really brag about."

"I hope so."

"You're two for two thus far," he reminded her.

She grinned and ran her pinky down his bare chest. "And I get you as a bonus."

He was only too happy for that. "I'm all yours to do with as you please."

"Are you sure you're ready for that?" Paula asked.

Chase considered the question. He'd been alone longer than he cared to be. He didn't want to go back to those dark and dreary days, not when there was someone who had suddenly given his life new meaning, filling him with optimism.

"I'm ready," he promised, pausing. "Are you?"

Paula unbuttoned the shirt and allowed it to fall to the floor, revealing her graceful nakedness. She moved closer, rubbing herself against him. "Does that answer your question?"

He grinned. "Sure does."

"Thought so," she cooed and puckered her lips.

Chase kissed Paula's waiting lips. He sucked hungrily on her lower lip and slid his tongue in her mouth, searching till he found her tongue. "I can't seem to ever get my fill of you."

"Hmm…" She pressed her breasts against his chest. "Then you'll just have to keep coming back for more."

"I sure will." He kissed her again, taking delight in the meeting of their mouths before needing even more to satisfy his growing appetite for the lady.

Chase carried Paula to the couch and laid her down. Dropping to his knees, he held her breasts, which were like well-rounded, beautiful melons. The nipples were taut and tempting. He ran his tongue across one, then the other, and back again. Chase focused entirely on one nipple, wrapping his lips around it and sucking, then licking. Paula's breathing quickened and her body trembled. He moved to the other nipple and did the same as she reacted, causing his libido to soar.

"That feels so good," she uttered. "So very good…."

Chase continued to kiss her breasts and nipples, getting more and more aroused. He wanted to take it to another level for them. He moved down Paula's appealing, smooth body, peppering her flesh with kisses, leaving chill bumps in his wake. Opening Paula's thighs, Chase homed in on the triangle of dark, curly hair. He touched her moist clitoris, gently moving his fingertip back and forth. She tensed and murmured. He put his face there and inhaled her tantalizing scent, stirring his emotions. She was wet, and he began licking her. His mouth covered her most sensitive spot, and he used his tongue expertly, provoking cries of appeasement from Paula.

Chase clutched her quivering body while continuing to flick his tongue. He flinched as Paula dug her fingernails into his shoulders. She moaned loudly when the peak of her climax claimed her. Chase enjoyed gratifying Paula and was now ready to satisfy her again.

He lifted up, and she held his cheeks with trembling hands. "Give me your lips," she pleaded urgently.

Chase was only too happy to oblige, for he needed the fullness and joy of her mouth upon his at this moment even more.

The next day, Paula was home alone while Isabelle was visiting a friend. She'd thought about phoning Chase to come over for some fun and frolic in bed, but didn't want the man to think she was a raging sex maniac.

Or was it more the other way around?

Whatever the case, Paula cherished the intimate time they were spending together and had come to believe that she might actually have found someone to build a future with. Maybe that diamond ring on her finger was no longer just a fantasy with little chance of ever coming true. Chase could be the man who would one day pop the question. She had a good idea what the answer would be, too, given the way she was starting to feel about him.

Her reverie was broken when Paula heard the doorbell ring. She went downstairs and opened the door. Standing there was her ex, Sheldon Burke.

"Hello," he said, standing tall in a black pinstripe suit that filled his husky frame nicely.

She frowned with annoyance. "What are you doing here?"

He brushed aside his dreadlocks. "I came to see you."

"There's nothing left to say." Paula wanted to make that perfectly clear.

Sheldon's nostrils flared. "I disagree. There were a few things left unsaid when you decided to just end our relationship out of the blue. I only want to clear the air." He paused, looking at her. "You owe me that much."

Paula eyed him warily. Her first instinct was to not add fuel to the fire by giving in to his request, but she feared he'd simply keep harassing her if she ignored him. She preferred to get this over with once and for all.

"You've got five minutes," she said tersely, glancing at her watch.

Sheldon walked past Paula coolly and went into the living room. She followed him, deciding not to ask him to sit down.

Paula put her hand on her hip. "So, what do you have to say?"

"Did Isa tell you I dropped by the other day?" Sheldon asked.

"Yes, she mentioned it."

"I tried calling you, too, more than once. I even sent you a couple of text messages."

"I know," Paula said, realizing there was no need to say otherwise. "I've been really busy."

He rolled his eyes. "Yeah, haven't we all."

She looked at her watch. "The clock is ticking…." *Maybe it was a mistake to let him in.*

Sheldon walked up to her and put his arms around her waist. "I've missed you…. Missed us."

Paula could smell alcohol on his breath. "I haven't missed you, and there is no us." She removed his hands and backed away. "I thought I made my feelings very clear. It's pointless to rehash this."

"That's not how I see it." He took a step toward her. "We were really great together."

"We were never that great together," she retorted honestly. "We tried to make it work, but we just weren't clicking."

"You say that now, but I never heard any complaints from you before, especially in bed."

Paula curled her lip. She wondered now how she had ever allowed him to touch her. "I guess that was my mistake," she spat. "Now, if you're done, I'd like you to leave."

Sheldon frowned. "If you wanted out, why didn't you just say it to my face instead of leaving me a damned voice mail?"

She sighed. "You know perfectly well that I left the voice mail only *after* you refused to listen to what I was telling you face-to-face. I simply didn't want it to become confrontational. I never meant to hurt you. I just felt we were better off going our separate ways."

"I don't agree with that," he said tersely.

Paula backed away from him. "We can agree to disagree. Either way, it's over between us and has been for a while now."

"Are you seeing someone else?" Sheldon asked point-blank.

Paula thought about her relationship with Chase and wondered if it would help or hurt her cause by making it part of the conversation. She decided Sheldon was only trying to stir up trouble, which she wanted no part of.

"That's none of your business," she responded tartly.

"I'll take that as a yes."

Paula held her ground. "Take it any way you like."

Sheldon sneered. "Is that why you broke up with me, so you could be with another man?"

Paula blinked. She would not allow herself to be intimidated by him, and she certainly wouldn't let him make her feel guilty, knowing that their relationship had been completely over before she ever laid eyes on Chase.

"You've been drinking."

He ran his hand across his mouth. "Can you blame me? I thought we had something. Then you just leave me high and dry."

She scowled. "Let's get real here. You're a nice-looking guy and successful, too. If I bruised your ego, I'm sorry. I'm sure there are plenty of other single, available women you can hook up with if you want to."

Sheldon reached out and touched her face. "That's just it. I don't want anyone but you."

Paula slapped his hand away. "You can't have me."

"You're sure about that?" he challenged.

"I think you know the answer." She could feel her heart racing. "Your five minutes are up. You need to leave now!"

Sheldon grunted, stepping closer to her. "This isn't over."

Paula cringed, seeing the coldness in his eyes. "You're scaring me."

He took a breath, and his features softened. "I'm not going to hurt you. I just want us to—"

The front door opened at that moment, and Isabelle came in. She raised a brow when she saw Sheldon.

"What is he doing here?" she asked nervously.

Paula locked eyes with her ex. "He was just leaving. Weren't you?"

Sheldon contorted his lips. "Yeah, I was."

"Have a nice day," Isabelle told him tartly. "Don't let the door hit you on the way out."

He looked at Paula with a hard gaze. "See you later."

She said nothing in response, hoping his words were merely a figure of speech. Obviously, any chance of them remaining platonic friends had ended today. He had seen to that.

After Sheldon left, Isabelle asked Paula with concern, "Are you all right?"

"Yes." Paula felt her nerves begin to calm down. "I thought if I let him say his piece, he'd leave me alone."

"So what did he want?"

"To get back together," Paula moaned.

Isabelle grimaced. "What did you tell him?"

"What I've told him before—that it's over for good." She drew a breath. "It just goes in one ear and out the other."

"The man's becoming a stalker," Isabelle asserted. "Can you get a restraining order before he does something really stupid, if not downright dangerous?"

"I think he got the message," Paula said unevenly. After all, she had given it to him straight this time, whether he liked it or not; the Sheldon she knew was not foolhardy when it came to assessing the situation squarely.

Isabelle batted her lashes dubiously. "And what if he hasn't? You can't live your life in fear, wondering when he'll show up next."

"I know that."

Paula wondered if Sheldon could be dangerous. She wanted to believe he was just blowing off steam as his way of dealing with rejection. He had never really displayed jealousy or aggression during their relationship, so where was this coming from now?

She didn't want any of this to spill over to her involvement with Chase. The last thing she needed was for him to see her as wishy-washy, or playing with a man's emotions. The reality was, she'd been looking all her adult life for a man like Chase. He had the right combination of good looks, strong character, sex appeal, hard work ethic and old-fashioned values that spoke to her.

Hopefully, Sheldon would turn his attention to someone else, and she could continue her romance with Chase without unwanted distractions. Sheldon would just have to accept that their relationship was over.

Chapter 11

Chase made the rounds of McCord Diamonds' jewelry stores, checking inventory, assessing needs and giving a pep talk to employees. They were now in the midst of the holiday season, and despite a struggling economy, diamonds and other precious gemstones remained popular items to purchase. In fact, Chase expected the sales figures for this year to be better than ever. It was something he hoped to build on in the future by introducing new products and having an aggressive sales campaign.

Back in his car, Chase headed for the office with Antwerp on his mind. He would be making the trip to Belgium next week. He wondered if it was too soon to ask Paula to accompany him on such a journey. Yes, they seemed to be establishing a real relationship that was bordering on serious, but was he ready to take her to the land of diamonds for a romantic getaway separate from his business trip? Maybe she wasn't ready to take things to such a level until they got to know each other better outside of their sexual relationship.

I don't want to mess things up or take away from the strides we've already made.

Chase also didn't want to sit back and let life pass him by. Rochelle's death had proven to him that you had to make every minute count, for the future was always in doubt. With Paula, he wanted to embrace the present and experience as much as they could together. That included spending time away from their comfort zone. But she had to want it, too. Wherever they were headed, it would take the two of them to make it work.

Chase pulled into his private parking space in the garage. He checked his cell phone and noted that Paula had sent him a text message.

Hi. Thinking about u. Call me. P.

A smile crossed his face. He couldn't help but recall their last hot and heavy sexual escapade. Everything about Paula was driving his libido crazy.

He punched her number on his speed dial.

"Hey, there," she said in a sugary voice.

"Hey. I got your message."

"What are you up to?" Paula asked.

"I just got back from visiting some of our stores," Chase told her.

"I see. So you go around checking on everyone to make sure no one's slacking off on the job?"

He chuckled. "Yeah, something like that."

"And did you make anyone sit in the corner?" Paula teased.

Chase laughed, loving her sense of humor. "Fortunately, it didn't come to that."

She chuckled. "That's good."

"Are you working today?" he asked.

"Nope. Not officially, anyway. I'm just hanging out with Isa."

"I'd love to meet your grandmother sometime, if I'm not being too presumptuous," Chase said.

"I'd like that, too," Paula said keenly. "And I know Isa wants to meet you. I'll talk to her, and we'll set up a meeting."

"Sounds good." He saw this as a perfect opportunity to set up his own introduction. "Speaking of which, I'd like you to meet my best friend."

"Oh, I'd love to. Just name the time and place."

"My house on Wednesday at seven."

"I'll be there," Paula promised.

Chase smiled. "Great."

"By then, I should have some ideas on paper for your den."

"I'm sure you'll come up with something that will transform it into another room I'll want to spend more time in."

"It seems to me that you already found a good way to make use of it yesterday," Paula said.

Chase grinned thoughtfully. "I'd say we both did."

"Any complaints?" Paula dared to ask.

He chuckled. "None whatsoever."

"Just checking."

"You're turning me on," Chase admitted.

She laughed softly. "You're insatiable."

"And you aren't?"

"You'll have to figure that one out for yourself."

"I'd rather figure it out with you in private," he replied in a lascivious tone of voice.

"I accept your challenge," Paula said with a giggle.

"That's sweet music to my ears."

"From the sound of it, I'd say you and your new beau are definitely in sync," Virginia said enviously, holding a basket of clean clothes.

Paula was sitting at Virginia's kitchen table. She'd just finished her conversation with Chase. "I didn't know you were listening."

"The dryer isn't that loud. Besides, with the cutesy lilt to your voice, it was obvious."

"Okay, you've got me," Paula admitted. "We were having a little fun."

Virginia put the basket down and wiped her brow. "There's nothing wrong with that. I wish I were so lucky."

She was between relationships, and Paula imagined it wouldn't be long before another man had hooked her.

"Your time will come," Paula told Virginia.

"Not soon enough," she complained.

"I thought the same thing not so long ago. Then things changed. I'm feeling pretty good these days."

Virginia grabbed her mug from the counter. "That's great."

"Chase definitely seems like he's ready to romance a woman," Paula said, sipping hot chocolate.

Virginia smiled. "And that would be you?"

"Yes, I'm happy to say." Then Paula's smile fell.

"Okay, so what aren't you telling me?"

"Nothing," Paula hedged.

Virginia peered at her. "Come on, I know you too well not to realize when something's up."

Paula sighed, deciding she needed to confide in her friend. "Sheldon stopped by my house earlier today."

"He what?"

"Said he wanted to 'clear the air,' so I let him in." Paula paused. "Big mistake."

Virginia sat down. "What happened?"

"He wanted to get back together."

"And I assume you told him where to go?"

"Yes, in so many words," Paula said. "Only he didn't want to listen. He'd been drinking, too."

"I never knew him to be much of a drinker," Virginia said. "Not that you have to be an alcoholic to overdo it."

Paula wrinkled her nose. "I don't think Sheldon was drunk, but that's not the point. He still made me uncomfortable."

"Did he try anything?" Virginia lowered her eyebrows with concern.

"Nothing happened, other than the fact he doesn't seem

to get that what we had is over. I'm just afraid of what he might do next."

"I'm sorry you ended up getting involved with someone who turned out to be such a jerk," Virginia said sourly.

"You and me both," said Paula, shifting in her chair. "I just want him to leave me alone so it doesn't spill over into my relationship with Chase."

"Have you told him about Sheldon?"

"I told Chase I had an ex who proved to be a mistake, without getting into specifics."

"Probably best to leave it at that," Virginia said and sipped her coffee. "No reason to dole out lurid details if Chase doesn't ask about them. The only thing that really matters is that Sheldon is strictly a thing of the past and Chase is hopefully a big part of your future."

"That's my way of thinking," Paula concurred. "For maybe the first time in my life, I think I might have found my true match with Chase. I just want us to have a fair chance to grow without anyone trying to mess things up."

"Do you want me to talk to Sheldon?" Virginia volunteered.

Paula knew that Virginia had known Sheldon before they met, albeit only casually. But should she have to intercede on her behalf?

"You don't have to—" Paula began, not wanting to get her friend involved.

"It's okay," Virginia insisted. "He has to get it in his head that you've moved on, and he should, too, for everyone's sake."

Paula touched Virginia's hand. "Thanks. I really appreciate this."

"I'm happy to do it for my best friend. If Sheldon wants to create problems, he'll have to take us both on."

Paula leaned over and hugged Virginia. She hoped to put Sheldon behind her once and for all so she could focus all her energy on the one and only man she really wanted to be with these days.

* * *

"This is Monica," Chase said to Paula. "She works with me, in addition to being a very good friend. And this is Zachary."

"Hi," Paula greeted them. She did a quick scan of the woman, finding her very attractive and nicely dressed in a black pantsuit and matching pumps. The man, in a dark suit, was well-built and bald.

Monica extended her hand. "It's nice to meet you, Paula. Chase has told me all about your decorating skills."

Paula shook her hand. "I suspect he went a little overboard," she said modestly.

"You can see for yourself," Chase said. "Check out the great room."

"Very nice," marveled Monica as she entered the room.

"Yeah, it is." Zachary nodded with appreciation.

"Thank you." Paula was tempted to hand out business cards but didn't want to make a bad first impression as someone who was only interested in seeking new clients.

"Can I get everyone something to drink?" Chase asked and went through the choices. The consensus was red wine. "Coming right up. In the meantime, everyone sit down and get comfortable."

Paula sat across from Monica and Zachary. She wondered how Monica and Chase had come to be such good friends.

"I understand you worked on Chase's father's house," Monica said.

Paula nodded. "Yes, I redecorated his recreation room."

"Maybe Chase and Sylvester will want you to do something with their corporate offices, too," Monica suggested.

"Have you worked there long?" Paula asked curiously.

"Yes, I'm the vice president," she replied. "And Zachary is a gemologist for one of our stores."

"I see." Paula glanced at him, and he smiled in return.

"It keeps me pretty busy," he said, "except for when this lady steals me away."

Monica laughed uncomfortably. "I wouldn't exactly call it stealing. More like borrowing."

"I stand corrected," Zachary said.

"He gets like this sometimes," Monica said with amusement. "Get used to it."

Paula chuckled. So they were an item and apparently spent their fair share of time around Chase for work and play. Paula noticed that Monica seemed to be sizing her up.

"Chase and I go back a long way," she said. "We lived in the same dorm in college and were once almost inseparable."

Paula contemplated that. Had their relationship always been platonic? And just how close were they today?

"So you were friends with his late wife, too?" Paula asked with interest.

"Yes. Rochelle was a wonderful lady and the love of Chase's life. He was devastated when she died."

"I'm sure he was." Paula wondered if this was Monica's attempt to try to undermine her relationship with Chase. Or was she trying to get under her skin?

"It's good to know that Chase is dating someone again who is not only gorgeous, but obviously very talented," Monica expressed. "I really hope things work out between you guys."

"Thank you," Paula said, coloring. "So do I." Monica obviously had Chase's best interests at heart.

Chase returned with the drinks and a tray with snacks. He was a little nervous about Monica meeting Paula, though not sure why. Probably because he wanted them to like each other, since they were both important people in his life. He'd also found Monica to be a good judge of character and sought reassurance from an old friend that his choice in Paula as a girlfriend was a wise one.

Chase sat next to Paula, feeling warmth emanating from her. "I hope Monica didn't inundate you with twenty questions."

"Not at all," she said.

"We're just getting to know each other," Monica chirped.

He grinned. "That's great."

"One nice, big, happy family," Zachary said with a laugh.

Chase studied him. He seemed like a nice guy, even though he didn't really know him. Was Zachary just a casual fling for Monica, or had she also found someone she could develop a serious relationship with?

Monica grabbed a pretzel. "I was just telling Paula that you and Sylvester might want to give our offices a makeover."

Chase wasn't opposed to the idea and was sure his father wouldn't object, given that he was the one who had bragged about Paula's work so much that Chase felt compelled to check her out for himself. It was perhaps one of the best moves he had ever made.

"That's certainly possible," he said with enthusiasm. "We'll have to look into it."

"I'd be glad to take a look around and offer some suggestions," Paula told him.

Chase sat back. "I'll let you know." He imagined that with her wonderfully creative mind, she could pretty much transform any space into a work of art. His greater focus at the moment was on building their personal relationship. He suspected Paula felt the same way.

"Do you like diamonds?" Monica asked Paula.

"What woman doesn't?" she replied wide-eyed over her wine goblet.

"If you're interested, I'll send you our latest catalog loaded with goodies, assuming Chase hasn't already given it to you."

"No, he hasn't." Paula angled her eyes at Chase admonishingly. "And, yes, I'd love to see your catalog."

Chase grinned sheepishly, wondering why he hadn't thought of this. He would be interested to know what types of diamonds or other gemstones Paula liked. It could be useful knowledge for him in the future.

"We try to stay on top of all the hot items," Chase said proudly, "as well as those that are enduring."

Zachary leaned forward. "If you or any of your family

members have some precious jewelry that needs to be recut, cleaned or inspected, I'll be happy to do it."

"Thanks," Paula said. "I just might take you up on that. My grandmother's wedding ring has certainly seen better days."

"We can definitely take care of that," Chase offered. He nodded at Zachary in appreciation for stepping up to the plate on behalf of Paula. Chase looked forward to meeting the woman who played such an important role in Paula's life.

"Can I get anyone a refill?" Chase asked, looking around.

By the time the get-together had come to an end, Chase was holding hands with Paula. It felt good to be able to share their affection in front of others, as Chase enjoyed socializing with friends and family. Having Paula in his life made the experience more meaningful again.

They walked Monica and Zachary outside. The night was chilly and clear.

While Paula was chatting with Zachary, Chase took a moment to whisper in Monica's ear. "So, what do you think of her?"

Monica smiled brightly with a thumbs-up. "I think you made a good choice. Don't let her get away."

"I'll try to hold on to her," Chase promised, happy for the support.

"Something tells me she feels just as strongly about you."

Chase took that to heart. As long as he and Paula were compatible and shared the same feelings about each other, Chase felt there was no limit to how far they could go.

Chapter 12

"You didn't tell me your best friend was such an attractive female," Paula said lightheartedly after Monica and Zachary had left.

Chase grinned as they stood in the den. "Truthfully, we've known each other so long that I hardly even think of her in terms of being female or attractive. She's just Monica."

Paula rolled her eyes. "Yeah, right."

He chuckled, holding her waist. "Are you jealous?"

"Should I be?"

"Not as far as I'm concerned. We're friends and colleagues. End of story."

"I believe you," Paula said, kissing him. She didn't consider herself to be the jealous type, but she was a woman, and most women were at least a little insecure when it came to their men being friends with other women, platonic or not. In this case, she liked Monica and would never try to come between her and Chase. She respected their long history. Besides, Monica seemed really into Zachary.

Paula removed her mouth from Chase's. "Satisfied?"

He touched his lips desirously. "It's a good start."

"We'll have to finish it a little later," she told him, disregarding the tingling sensation between her legs. "Right now I'd like to give you my ideas for this room."

"If you insist." Chase put his arm around her shoulders. "I'm all ears."

Paula gave the den a sweeping glance. "Well, for starters, I would replace the leather chairs with fabric furniture. Adding a reclining chaise might be nice for those days when you just want to lay back and watch TV or listen to music." She paused long enough to gauge his reaction, which seemed supportive. "A solid birch entertainment system with multiple cabinets and adjustable glass shelves would enable you to have all the electronics, CDs and DVDs in one convenient place. How does it sound so far?"

"Sounds great," Chase said sincerely. "You never fail to amaze me with your vision for redecorating a room."

Paula smiled, feeling spoiled by him and his generosity. "There's more. I'd love to add a curved casual table and some accent lamps. A hand-knotted contemporary rug would be the finishing touch to your new den."

He kissed her. "As usual, your plan is well-thought-out and incredible."

She licked her lips with buoyancy. "So, is it a go, then?"

"Yes, go, go, go and remake my den."

Paula beamed. "You're quickly becoming my most cherished client."

"Is that so?" Chase kissed her again. "I'd rather be your most cherished boyfriend."

"That, too." She gave him a lingering kiss. "Most definitely." Paula liked thinking of Chase as her boyfriend. It meant they had made the giant leap into the next chapter of their relationship, which was cause for celebration.

"So, what are we going to do to cement the deal?" Chase asked, reading her thoughts.

She gave him a seductive look. "Do you have to ask?"
He grinned lasciviously. "I think not."

Chase was lying on his side, cradling Paula's naked body with her back to him as they made love tempestuously. He felt her vagina squeeze around his penis deep within while his fingers gently rubbed her clitoris. Paula gasped from the intense pleasure, turning her face to seek out his waiting mouth. She kissed his lips, sucking them fervently and whipping her tongue in and out. Chase passionately returned the kiss, wrapping his tongue around hers.

They kissed feverishly, open mouths locked in motion as Chase thrust his erection into Paula, getting as much pleasure as he gave. He grunted as each contraction drew him deeper and deeper, holding him inside as if he were her love slave. He wanted nothing more than to be right where he was in exploring their sexuality and heated lust for one another.

Paula turned around and pulled Chase on top of her. She wrapped her legs around his thighs. Clutching his buttocks, she propelled herself upward, meeting his hard chest with her soft breasts.

Chase reciprocated, feeling her nipples brushing against him as he lowered himself, bringing their bodies even closer. He went after Paula's moist lips, nibbling them before kissing her zealously. He fought hard to suppress his orgasm, loving it when they came together. Chase's body quivered as he intensified his thrusts and Paula nibbled on his neck. He could feel her heart racing as surely as his was. They were both slick with sweat, stuck together in heated bliss as the sexual chemistry sizzled between them like an inferno.

"It's coming," Paula uttered into his mouth, gripping him tighter.

"Let yourself go." Chase's voice was ragged, his own needs threatening to overpower him.

"I will, all the way…."

Chase drove his penis into her frenetically, going as far as she would allow, his willpower slipping away till there was none left to stop the surge. He caught his breath while relishing the feeling of ecstasy and fulfillment. Paula cried out with unabashed delight as their intense spasms jolted them. They reached the summit in unison, overcome by the torrid response of their bodies as each seized every moment to bask in the afterglow of their intimacy.

"What was your wife like?" Paula asked as they sat wrapped in a blanket before crackling logs in the fireplace. She didn't want to make Chase uncomfortable, but she was curious about the woman he'd loved enough to marry.

Chase angled his head musingly. "Rochelle was a feisty, meticulous woman with a kind heart and loving soul. She loved musicals, gardening, old movies, baseball and reading historical novels."

"It sounds like she was into a variety of things."

"She was," Chase said thoughtfully. "Sometimes I had trouble just trying to keep up with her."

"Did she work outside the house?"

"Rochelle was an English professor until her deteriorating health made it impossible to work."

"How did she die?" Paula asked, wanting to know such things about the woman to whom Chase had first given his love.

"She had a heart defect," he said. "She'd been able to control it with medication for years, but it finally caught up with her."

Paula felt for Rochelle, being robbed of life so young and losing Chase, who was undoubtedly a wonderful and devoted husband. She surely didn't deserve such a fate. It made Paula feel slightly uneasy that she had stepped into Rochelle's shoes in Chase's life. She knew no one could ever replace his wife, and she did not want to. Paula could only be herself and let nature take its course with them.

"What are you thinking?" Chase asked, eyeing her beneath a furrowed brow.

Paula caught his gaze. "How sad her passing must have been for you."

"Yeah, it really tore me up for a long time, but I came to realize that we had ten great years together. That's more than a lot of couples ever have."

"That's true." None of Paula's relationships had lasted very long. Mainly it was because she hadn't found a man who could keep her interested, or who she could count on to be faithful and serious about trying to make things work. Paula sensed things were different with Chase, making her want to stick around to see where they were headed.

"Tell me about your last relationship," he said casually.

She widened her eyes, thoughtful. "What do you want to know?"

"You said the guy made you want to run and hide from all men."

Paula tensed. *I can't believe he remembered that.* "Yes, something like that."

"Just what did he do to turn you off so much?" Chase asked flatly.

She wondered how much she should say. She didn't want to go on and on about someone she'd just as soon forget, especially after the last episode with Sheldon left her wanting to run for the hills.

"He was too much into himself," she said frankly, "and too controlling. After a while, I realized that mainly he was just plain old boring."

Chase laughed. "I suppose boredom is as good a reason as any for ending a relationship."

Paula blinked her eyes. "I think so."

"And a good reason for starting another relationship," he suggested.

She smiled. "True."

Chase studied her. "I think you did the right thing to walk away."

"I know I did," she voiced emphatically.

"I'm just glad you were available to come into my life when you did."

She crinkled her eyes at him. "I can certainly say the same for you."

He smiled handsomely. "I guess timing is everything." He gave her a soft kiss.

Paula enjoyed the kiss, getting quite used to having his lips upon hers. "And just so we're clear, there's absolutely nothing boring about you."

Chase showed his teeth. "I'll try to keep it that way."

"I don't think you'll have to work very hard."

"That's half the fun," he suggested.

"And the other half?"

"This…"

Chase kissed her again, and Paula's toes curled delightfully as she kissed him back. She was thoroughly enthralled by the man. She doubted anyone had ever kissed her with such skill and passion.

"Did Rochelle want children?" Paula asked curiously once they finally broke away from each other.

Chase scratched his nose. "Yes, and so did I. We tried to get pregnant early on, but once she got sick, the strain a pregnancy would place on her became too risky."

Paula lowered her eyes. "I'm sorry you never got the chance to have a family. I know you would've been a great dad."

"I have to believe most things happen for a reason," he said in earnest. "I guess it wasn't meant to be at that time in my life."

Paula tried to read into that. Did he still want to have children? Did he want to marry again? She stared at the fire that was still going strong.

"How do you feel about kids?" Chase asked her.

Paula turned to face him. "I would love to have a child one day, after I'm married and settled into the relationship," she responded directly. "I know that would make my grandmother happy, too."

He grinned. "So she wouldn't mind chasing an energetic child all over the house at her age?"

"That shouldn't be too much of a problem." Paula chuckled. "Isa has more energy than some people twenty years younger."

"I guess it must run in the family," he said, eyeing her lasciviously.

She blushed and recalled their recent exercise in bed. "I could say the same for you."

Chase nodded. "Well, I do come from pretty good stock, at least on my father's side."

Paula didn't doubt it one bit. "I can see that." He cuddled her. She felt cozy in his arms. "By the way, my grandmother wanted me to ask if you could come to dinner on Friday night. She's doing the cooking."

"I'd love to."

"Bring your appetite. She usually makes enough to feed an army."

"I'll be sure to skip lunch that day," Chase said with a laugh.

Paula was eager for Chase and Isabelle to meet. Her grandmother had been quite intuitive where it concerned him. She'd like her firsthand impression.

Chase's hand moved to the spot between her legs. "I think I'm starting to get a good idea of what works for you."

She quivered. "Pretty confident in your skills, aren't you?"

"Well, I admit they hadn't been put to much good use recently," he said coolly. "Then you walked into my life, and things changed."

"I'm happy I could help you out." Paula was just as happy to be the recipient of his sexual prowess.

"So am I." Chase leaned over and gave her a tasty kiss. "Very glad." He ran his thumb across one nipple, then the other.

"Mmm."

"Feel good?"

Paula's eyes were closed. "Yes, very good," she said softly.

He put his hand between her thighs again. "How about that?"

She hummed. "I think you know the answer."

"I think I do," he said seductively. "In that case, we better do something about it."

Paula sighed with anticipation. "You've already gotten us started."

Chase moistened his lips. "And I always finish what I start."

He locked his mouth on to hers, and Paula ardently let herself go.

Chapter 13

"I'm going to ask Paula to go to Antwerp with me," Chase told his father while they worked out on treadmills at a health club.

Sylvester took a deep breath. "Sounds like things are getting serious between you two."

"Yeah, we're pretty tight right now. I feel like I've known her for years."

Sylvester peered at him. "You mean like Rochelle?"

Chase wiped his brow. "Rochelle was my wife, the love of my life."

"I know how you felt about her," Sylvester said. "I loved Rochelle like a daughter, but you're at a new point in your life now. If I'm reading you right, it sounds like you think there might be a future with Paula."

Chase nodded. He certainly wanted to believe that. He sensed that Paula wanted it, too. But he didn't want to jump the gun and get ahead of himself. Then it could backfire, leaving him back where he started: alone and unhappy.

"I'm a widower, and she's never been married," he told his father. "Do you think that could become an issue down the line?"

Sylvester shook his head. "Son, you're not the first man to lose his wife and find a new love. I'm sure a smart woman like Paula understands that and doesn't hold your misfortune against you any more than you do that she's never met anyone she wanted to marry."

"I can't say we've reached the point of love in our relationship," Chase hedged. "But I do want to pursue what we have to see where it leads."

"Then go for it. You deserve to be happy."

"Happy." Chase's brow creased. "That's not as easy as it sounds."

"It doesn't have to be hard," Sylvester said. "Life is about what you make it. Once Evelyn came into the picture, I put all my second thoughts and what-ifs behind me. You can do the same thing. And your old man will be there every step of the way for encouragement."

Chase grinned. "I appreciate that."

"I hope Paula agrees to go with you to Antwerp," Sylvester said, his face perspiring. "It's beautiful there at this time of year, not to mention very romantic."

"Yeah, it sure is—on both counts."

Chase was thoughtful as he began his workout cooldown, an image of Paula naked forming in his head.

Paula was a bundle of nerves as Chase came up the walkway. They had just spoken on the phone and exchanged sweet words. But now was the time for Chase and Isabelle to scope each other out.

"Hi," Paula said to Chase in an upbeat tone.

"Hey." A half grin played on his lips.

"Did you have any trouble finding the place?" she asked, suspecting he hadn't.

"Not at all," he confirmed. "Your directions were right on the money."

Paula kissed him on the mouth and then used her finger to wipe lip gloss away. She loved the cologne he wore, its spicy redolence. "Please come in."

They walked into the living room, where Isabelle was seated, trying to appear cool and calm.

"Chase, this is my grandmother, Isabelle."

"Call me Isa," she said, sticking out her hand. "It's much less formal."

"Nice to meet you, Isa." Chase shook her hand.

"Welcome to our home."

"Happy to be here." He gazed down at her. "I see you have an accent."

"That's right."

"South African?"

Isabelle smiled. "Yes, South African English. I grew up in Johannesburg. Afrikaans is my native language."

Chase nodded with recognition. "I knew someone in college from South Africa who spoke Afrikaans and Zulu. He lived in Soweto."

"I have distant relatives in that part of Johannesburg," Isabelle informed him. "Have you been there?"

"My friend once invited me to come to Soweto, but I never made it," Chase said. "I'd still love to visit South Africa someday, especially with its diamond-mining industry and history, along with its cultural diversity and multiple languages."

"You certainly get an A for linguistics," Paula pitched in with amusement, happy to see him with an interest in her grandmother's homeland.

Chase chuckled. "Actually, I fell a little short of that in school, but I did pick up a few South African words from my friend."

"I've heard a lot about you, young man," Isabelle said.

Chase lifted his hands in a playful defensive posture. "I hope Paula was kind."

Isabelle's eyes creased when she smiled. "She's had nothing but good things to say."

He sighed. "Oh, good. I can breathe easily now."

Isabelle chuckled, and Paula could see that these two would get along just fine.

"Do you want to sit down?" Paula asked Chase.

"Sure," he said.

Isabelle climbed to her feet. "You two can wash up and sit in the dining room. The food's about ready."

"Can I help with anything?" asked Chase.

"This is a real gentleman you've got here, Paula." Isabelle paused and looked at Chase. "You're our guest, so I'll manage on my own."

Paula cupped her arm under Chase's. "There's no arguing with her," she told him.

"Guess not." Chase waited for Isabelle to disappear into the kitchen before gazing down at Paula. "How am I doing so far?"

"You're doing great. I think Isa likes you. In fact, she's liked you practically from the moment I first told her about you."

"That reminds me of a certain someone who was clearly keen on you from day one," Chase said.

"Your father?" she presumed.

"Yeah. Dad has a real knack for that sort of thing."

Paula batted her eyes. "What sort is that?"

"Oh, beauty, brains, intellect, talent—just the run-of-the-mill stuff."

She laughed, enjoying teasing him. "So now you're saying I'm just run-of-the-mill?"

"Not in my book," Chase said firmly. "The main point is, while it's great to know that our families are on board with our relationship, it's more important that *we* like each other."

Paula's eyes glistened as she looked into his eyes. "Yes, we certainly do," she admitted.

They were halfway to the dining room when the doorbell rang. Paula jumped, fearing Sheldon had made a second unexpected visit. The last thing she needed was Sheldon to make a scene, especially after she'd made it perfectly clear that she wanted nothing more to do with him.

"Expecting company?" asked Chase.

Paula faced him. "No, we're not. Why don't you have a seat in the dining room, and I'll get rid of whoever it is."

She gave Chase a faint smile and watched him go into the dining room. Her heart skipped a beat as she peeked through the spy hole and opened the door. Paula breathed a sigh of relief when she saw Virginia standing there.

"Surprise!" Virginia said with a grin.

"Yes, it is," Paula agreed. Virginia normally called before dropping by.

"Is he here?" Virginia asked eagerly.

"Who?" Paula cocked a mystified brow.

"Mr. Diamond Man, who else?" Virginia replied.

Paula had forgotten she'd told her that Chase was coming for dinner. "Yes, he's here."

"So do I get to meet him?" Virginia pleaded. "I promise I'll be a good girl and won't stay long."

Paula couldn't exactly turn down her request. It was an opportune time for Virginia and Chase to finally meet. After all, Paula had already met Chase's friend, Monica, and wanted him to get to know her best friend, too.

"Of course," Paula told her. "And I'm holding you to keeping it short and sweet this time around."

"I understand," Virginia said, whisking past her. "So, where is the man?"

Paula led Virginia to the dining room, where Chase looked lonesome sitting by himself.

"Chase, this is my good friend Virginia," Paula said.

He rose and shook her hand. "How are you?"

"I'm great, thanks." Virginia studied him up and down. "Girl, you didn't exaggerate one bit. He's one fine, gorgeous hunk of man!"

Chase was speechless.

"He's also spoken for," Paula reminded her.

"I know," Virginia said with a grin. "I wouldn't dream of going after your man. But if he had a twin brother…"

"Sorry, there's only one of me," Chase said with amusement.

Paula was glad she had landed this one-of-a-kind man as her boyfriend and would do whatever was necessary to keep him.

Isabelle entered the dining room, holding a plate of food. "I thought I heard another voice."

"Hi, Isa," Virginia said.

"Hello, Virginia." Isabelle beamed. "You're just in time for dinner."

Paula didn't want Virginia to stay. She wanted this gathering to be all about Chase and Isabelle. There would be plenty of time later for Virginia to drool over him. She eyed her friend, making sure she got the message again.

"It smells fantastic," Virginia told Isabelle, "but I can't stay. I just dropped by to say hello."

"Oh, that's too bad. Maybe next time you can stay longer?" Isabelle winked at Paula, indicating she understood.

"Nice meeting you, Chase," Virginia told him.

"You, too," he said with an awkward wave.

Paula showed her friend to the door.

"Looks like you really hit the jackpot with Chase," Virginia said spiritedly.

Paula grinned. "I think so, too."

"Call me with all the juicy details on how the evening goes," Virginia chirped. "Or as many details as you care to share."

"I'll do that."

Paula gave Virginia a hug, closed the front door after Virginia left and returned to the dining room.

"Nice friend you've got there," Chase remarked.

"I think the feelings are mutual," she said with a smile, running her hand along the side of his face.

He smiled and pulled Paula onto his lap. "That's her problem."

Paula batted her eyes at him. "Says who?"

"Says me."

Chase kissed Paula, and she kissed him back just long enough to keep her on his mind.

"You're right," she said, her lips tingling. "It's totally Virginia's problem."

"I thought you'd see things my way," he said confidently.

Paula laughed playfully. "What other way is there?"

"How about your way?"

"We'll have to negotiate the terms," she teased. "At the appropriate time, of course."

Chase gave her a broad smile. "Yeah, let's do that."

Paula stood up just as Isabelle was bringing another course into the room.

"I understand you're in the diamond business," Isabelle said to Chase from her spot at the head of the table.

He buttered a biscuit. "That's right."

"I imagine this must be a pretty good time of the year for you, or has the economy messed that up?"

"There's no doubt that times are tough for everyone." His brow creased. "In spite of that, diamond sales are still holding their own. The holiday season accounts for the majority of our sales annually."

Isabelle touched the wedding band on her finger. "My late husband, Earl, proposed to me on Christmas Day many years ago. I still remember the joy and love I felt in that moment as if it were only yesterday."

"That's nice," Chase said, eyeing the ring. "You certainly can't beat a Christmas gift like that."

Isabelle's eyes twinkled. "That's a fact."

Chase grinned. "Earl obviously knew a good woman when he saw her and made sure she didn't get away."

Isabelle chuckled mirthfully. "That's sweet of you to say."

"Hey, I'm just telling like it is."

Paula enjoyed watching them interact. She could see that Isabelle was clearly moved by Chase's ability to tug at her heartstrings, making Paula even more impressed by the man. He was a true romantic.

"Isa, Chase and I talked about having your ring cleaned and repairing any damage it might have," Paula added.

Isabelle looked at Chase. "You can do that?"

"Sure. It would definitely sparkle like new when we were done."

She tried to twist the ring and move it. "I haven't taken it off in some time. I'm afraid it might be stuck in its place forever."

"We can take care of that for you," Chase assured her, slicing off a piece of roast beef, "and I promise you won't feel a thing."

Isabelle looked at Paula as though wondering if she should agree to it.

"Go for it," she told her grandmother. "Imagine how much you can relive your memories then whenever you look at your sparkling wedding ring."

Isabelle touched the ring. "I'd like that very much."

"Then we'll do it with my compliments," Chase told her.

Isabelle's face lit up. "He's definitely a keeper, Paula."

"Let's not embarrass the man," Paula said.

"Who says I'm embarrassed?" Chase uttered over a glass of wine. "As far as I'm concerned, we're both keepers."

Paula warmed at the notion. "I'm glad you feel that way," she told him gratefully. "I feel the same."

"I'm happy for you both," Isabelle said. "So tell me, Chase, apart from the physical attraction, did Paula do a good job working on your home?"

Chase nodded. "She did a fantastic job. Your granddaughter works wonders redecorating rooms."

Isabelle smiled proudly. "She certainly worked hard enough to educate and prepare herself for the profession."

"It certainly paid off," he said.

"Oh, yes, just look around you. Every room has examples of her handiwork."

"All right you two, enough already," Paula interjected. "You're going to make me conceited."

"Don't be afraid to take credit where it's due, child," Isabelle said.

"I agree." Chase flashed a toothy grin, seemingly amused by the whole thing.

Isabelle clasped her hands. "Would anyone like seconds? There's plenty of food left."

"It was delicious, but I think I'll hold the line there," said Chase, dabbing a napkin at the corners of his mouth.

"Me, too," seconded Paula. She didn't want to eat more than her man. She also wanted to maintain her svelte figure. Though she'd been blessed with a good metabolism, Paula had no intention of abusing that gift.

"Well, I hope you both saved a little room for a slice of apple pie," Isabelle said. "It's homemade."

Chase leaned back in his chair. "I love apple pie. I think I can manage one slice."

Paula felt that the dinner date couldn't have gone any better. Chase knew how to punch all the right buttons, which explained why she liked him more with each passing day.

Chase had his arm around Paula's shoulders as they sat in the movie theater, watching a romantic comedy. Her head rested comfortably on his chest. It was a relaxing way to spend quality time together after a wonderful meal and some quality conversation.

Chase was glad Paula's friend Virginia had stopped by, amusing and flattering him at the same time. He welcomed the opportunity to get to know the people who were important in Paula's life. It was a good way to get to know her better. This was especially true where it concerned her grandmother. Hearing Isabelle talk about Paula with such love and devotion was refreshing. It told him much of what he already knew: Paula was a beautiful, bright and vivacious woman that any man would be fortunate to have.

Chase knew he couldn't have found a more compatible person to be involved with at this point in his life. Paula, with her energy, passion, intelligence, openness and beauty, had given him reason to move forward rather than dwell on the past. She had brought out in him the fortitude to be the ardent, easygoing, spontaneous, romantic man he'd always been but had lost somewhere along the way. It reminded Chase that he had a whole lot of living left to do. Now he had met a lady who seemed just as vivacious. That was enough in and of itself to think positively about the promise of a future with her. If things worked out right, he couldn't see how she could say no to Antwerp.

Chapter 14

Paula felt like a teenager on a date with the hottest guy in school. She loved romantic movies and had finally found a man who loved them, too. Chase was the kind of man every woman dreamed about but was often out of reach or unavailable. Paula wondered how she had gotten so lucky.

As they sat in the middle of a darkened theater, sharing popcorn and a few kisses, Paula tried to focus on the movie again. It was about a newly single woman who meets two eligible bachelors on a cruise ship and finds herself pursued by both. But what she really wants is to get back with her ex beau, who, unbeknownst to her, has also come aboard the ship with the intention of proposing to her. It made for a hilarious story where love would somehow conquer all.

At the moment, Paula was more in tune with her own real-life romance. It was something she had not seen coming when she'd first laid eyes on Chase. Yet now she couldn't picture him not being in her life and giving her every reason to believe they were just getting started in building something with no end in sight.

Paula was still in a dreamy state by the time Chase pulled up in front of her house. "Thanks for the movie and for being so nice to my grandmother," she told him genuinely.

"The movie allowed me to spend more time with you," he said, his voice lowering an octave. "I didn't want to see the evening end too soon."

"Neither did I," she admitted.

Chase put his hand on her bare knee. "As for Isa, I was glad to finally meet her."

"I know she felt the same about you."

"Isa reminds me of my grandmother on my father's side, who spoiled me rotten when I was young," Chase said.

Paula batted her lashes. "Are you saying I'm spoiled?"

Chase laughed. "Not at all. I'm only saying that Isa is devoted to you, as any grandmother should be."

"You're right about that. She's been there for all my ups and downs. I don't know how I would've managed without her."

"It's great that Isa has been your rock, but the woman I've come to know has an independent streak in her a mile long and a cool head that would surely have seen you through whatever challenges you faced."

Paula's cheeks lifted into a smile. "I got that little independent streak from Isa."

Chase nodded. "I figured out that much. It doesn't change the fact that you're terrific."

She blushed. "You are so good for my confidence."

"That's just a fringe benefit of what we have going on here," Chase said smoothly.

"I'll take every fringe benefit you care to offer." Paula could think of a few such benefits that were already starting to raise her temperature a few notches.

"I'm happy you feel that way," Chase told her, "since I've got another one to throw at you."

"Oh?" She studied his face in the soft glow of the street-light. "Go right ahead. I'll try to catch whatever it is."

Chase smiled faintly before becoming serious. He took her hands. "I'm traveling to Antwerp, Belgium, next Thursday for business."

"Really?" She met his eyes.

"It's considered the world diamond center, boasting the finest diamonds and craftsmanship around. In what's known as the Antwerp Diamond Square Mile, there are over fifteen hundred international diamond companies, diamond-grading laboratories and much more! If you're in the diamond business, this is the place to wheel and deal. I'll be looking to shore up our spring and summer collections, as well as make a few purchases for current customers." He paused. "I'd like you to come with me."

Paula gave him a wide-eyed look. "Wow! Belgium." She'd never been there before, but was sure she would like it, especially in his company. "I'm flattered you're inviting me, but it's kind of short notice."

"I know, and I'm sorry about that. Our relationship seems like it's in a good place now. Antwerp is known as the city of romance as much as it is for its diamond trade. It has some of the finest international cuisine in the world, a historic old town, trendy nightlife and then some. We'd have a great time!"

"Sounds exciting," admitted Paula.

"It is, trust me," Chase promised. "Say you'll go."

The offer was almost too irresistible for Paula to turn down. Going anywhere with Chase was like a dream come true. Still, it was less than a week away, and she did have her business to consider. Not to mention trying to decide everything from how to wear her hair to what clothes to bring. And there was Isa to consider; Paula was concerned about leaving her alone.

"How long do you plan to stay?" she asked him.

"Three to four days. That should give us plenty of time to spend together doing as much as we can." He tilted his head. "And if you're wondering what to do to keep busy while I'm buying diamonds, you're more than welcome to accompany me. Or, better yet, you might want to use the opportunity to do some shopping. Antwerp has boutiques that carry some of the top designers' fashions."

"You make it very hard to pass up," Paula said softly.

He grinned slyly. "That's the whole point. Saying no is not an option."

She met his eyes. "You're so wonderful."

"Can I take that as a yes?" Chase was hopeful.

"Can I have a day to think about it? I have work and Isa to consider."

He smiled, rubbing her hand. "Of course. I understand that you have a life and responsibilities. Even if I'd really love to have your company in Antwerp, I don't want you to feel that saying no will be a game changer as far as what's happening between us."

"I don't," she told him, knowing it was a sweet gesture and a clear indication that he thought enough of her to extend the invitation. "And thank you."

Paula leaned over and gave Chase a long kiss, slipping her tongue in his mouth. She lost herself in the sweet taste of Chase's lips and the protection of his strong arms enveloping her. Paula never thought she would find a man who not only "got" her, but also opened up enough to allow her to "get" him. Yet that was precisely what she had gotten with Chase McCord, and she definitely would never take that for granted. The idea of being whisked away to a romantic paradise in Antwerp was gaining steam with every second that their mouths burned with impassioned harmony.

When Paula went inside, she found her grandmother still up watching TV.

"How was the movie?" Isabelle asked.

"Wonderfully romantic and funny."

"Glad you liked it, though I'm sure a lot of that had to do with the company."

Paula smiled thoughtfully. "More like all of it."

"No surprise there," Isabelle declared. "Your gentleman jeweler certainly left a favorable impression on me."

"Oh, really?" Paula teased her. "I hadn't noticed."

"He seems to be the complete package as far as I can tell."

"Yes, he certainly is," Paula concurred, if such a person really existed. She couldn't be more pleased that she had finally introduced Isa to someone neither of them could find fault with. There was no doubt in Paula's mind that the magical spell Chase had weaved so masterfully over her could potentially last a lifetime. "By the way, that complete package just invited me to go to Belgium with him next week."

"What?" Isabelle sat up. "Are you serious?"

"Yep." Paula beamed. "He's going to Antwerp to buy diamonds for his stores and wants to turn the trip into a romantic escape for a few days."

"That sounds wonderful. I take it you told him yes?"

Paula paused. "I told him I needed a day to think about it."

Isabelle frowned, creasing her brow. "What's to think about, child? He's offering you the world, or at least a very nice part of it."

"I don't want to have to worry about you while I'm being romanced in Europe," Paula told her.

"Then don't," Isabelle snapped. "I'm perfectly capable of taking care of myself for a few days. If I need help, I can call my friend Frances. Besides, I would feel terrible if you missed out on something so special because of me. I want you to put yourself first for once."

Paula smiled lovingly. She should have known Isabelle would not allow her to use this as an excuse to miss out on the trip of a lifetime.

"And that means first ahead of your job," Isabelle continued. "I know you have work lined up and clients who want to monopolize your time. They will still be around when you get back. However, good men like Chase don't come along every day, and they also don't need to put themselves out there if the woman plays hard to get."

Paula frowned. "I would never do that to Chase."

"Good. Then it's settled. You're going to Antwerp, and I'll hold the fort here till you get back."

Paula grinned, knowing her grandmother had cleverly made her see the light as always. "Okay, you win. I'll go."

"No, you and Chase win," Isabelle said magnanimously. "You have your whole lives ahead of you, so don't waste a moment. Believe me, it can all end way too soon."

Paula leaned over and gave Isa a big hug, aware she was referring to her true love who had been taken away prematurely, and perhaps to the loss Chase had experienced. The thought was sobering to Paula.

The next morning, Paula went running in the park. She ignored the cold breeze whipping at her face in favor of the adrenalin rush she got from pushing herself to go the extra mile. Paula was halfway to her goal and thinking about Chase when she heard the familiar voice from behind.

"I thought I'd find you here."

Her pulse missed a beat as she watched Sheldon pull up alongside her. Where had he come from?

Paula managed to keep her cool. "You're stalking me now?"

"Not at all," he said. "Remember we used to run together."

"That was then," she told him.

"Well, I'm still doing my thing every day."

"Good for you," Paula uttered sarcastically, resisting the temptation to run in a different direction. "If this is your attempt at a repeat of what's already been said, then—"

"Who's the dude?" Sheldon asked point-blank, keeping pace with her.

She stared at him, pretending to be mystified. "What are you talking about?"

"The man you were with last night," Sheldon said irritably.

Paula grew alarmed. "So you *are* stalking me?"

"Wrong again," he claimed. "I saw you at the theater when I was there with my date."

Paula wasn't sure she believed him, but hoped he had found a reason to leave her alone. "In that case, I don't think we have anything left to talk about," she said tartly.

"You still didn't answer my question," he pressed.

Nor did she want to, but if that was what it took to get this over with, Paula decided to satisfy his curiosity. "We're seeing each other, as if you haven't already guessed."

"Yeah, I figured as much." Sheldon took a breath. "So, did you do some work for him, too?"

Paula swallowed. How she'd met Chase was irrelevant. They could have become involved anywhere. The fact that she'd met Sheldon under similar circumstances after Virginia passed along that he was looking for an interior decorator was purely coincidental. It hardly meant a pattern or anything, as Paula's other boyfriends had nothing to do with her profession.

"That's none of your business," she said sharply.

He chuckled snidely. "Yeah, that's what I figured. And I'm sure you'll drop him like a hot potato, too, as soon as you set your pretty little eyes on someone else who comes along."

Paula had had just about as much of this as she could take. He had no right passing judgment on her, or pretending to be the wounded party. She stopped running, prompting him to do the same, and faced him squarely.

"You need to grow up!" Her voice shook. "When our relationship ended, I wasn't seeing another man."

Sheldon wiped his forehead. "And I'm supposed to believe that?"

Paula's brows knitted. "Believe whatever you want. I don't really care. I'm through playing these silly games with you, though. We broke up. That's what couples do when it's not working. So get over it and stop hounding me."

He backed off, as though pushed. "You've got it! I'm done."

"Thank you," Paula offered, for lack of anything more to say. "Now, if you don't mind, I'd like to finish my run—alone."

"Don't let me stop you."

She met his unreadable gaze and took off, half expecting

him to follow. He didn't, and she assumed that he'd finally gotten the message.

Paula sucked in a deep breath. She was glad that they had been able to settle this. Why were men so sensitive and downright hostile when it came to being the one dumped instead of the other way around? Why shouldn't it be a woman's prerogative to know when a relationship was going nowhere?

Paula couldn't imagine ever wanting to say goodbye to Chase, not when the man's kisses caused her heart to flutter wildly and her body temperature to rise to dangerous levels. That didn't even include his many other qualities. She couldn't wait to travel with him to Antwerp.

Chapter 15

Chase was up bright and early for a workout before showering, eating some oatmeal and going to the office. He wondered if it had been a mistake to ask Paula to accompany him to Antwerp. Maybe their relationship hadn't developed enough to expect her to toss aside any plans she may have had with little time to spare. He would rather have her go because she wanted to rather than just to please him.

The mouthwatering kiss they had shared when they said their goodbyes last night told Chase that Paula was definitely as much into him as he was her. But that didn't mean she was ready to move into uncharted waters in their burgeoning relationship. It was a big step for him, too. The only woman he'd ever taken to Belgium was Rochelle, so it would feel a bit strange to be there with another woman. It felt right, though, to invite Paula, since she had blended into his life in a way that made him want to experience as much as possible with her. He could only hope she felt the same way at the end of the day.

Sitting at his desk, Chase shared these sentiments with

Monica. He felt if anyone would understand, it would be her, since she had traveled to Antwerp with and without companionship.

"Don't sweat it, she'll go," Monica said flatly while sipping coffee.

"How can you be so sure?" Chase was curious, particularly when he wasn't nearly as certain.

Monica rolled her eyes. "What woman in her right mind would pass up a romantic excursion to the diamond capital of the world?"

"Maybe someone like Paula who has her business to consider. She's also responsible for her seventy-one-year-old grandmother who lives with her," Chase said. "And Paula doesn't strike me as a woman who is easily impressed with diamonds."

"Trust me when I say that diamonds leave an impression on every woman, no matter what kind of life she has." Monica sighed. "I don't know Paula very well, but it's pretty clear to me that she's crazy about you. With the holiday spirit in the air and romance blooming, spending time together in a faraway land is something she's equally excited about."

"Then why I am I still waiting for an answer?" Chase scratched his jaw. "I thought I asked her at the perfect moment, but apparently not."

Monica laughed. "You still don't know women very well, do you?"

He cocked a brow. "What don't I know?"

"That we like to keep you in suspense. It's part of our nature to not always agree right on the spot to things, no matter how tempting."

"That doesn't make sense." Chase shook his head.

"Doesn't have to, not to you anyway," she said. "The point is, it's our way of making you sweat it out so you don't take us for granted."

Chase grinned. "So that's all there is to it, huh?"

"Hey, take it from a woman who's been there, done that, with men for years. It's not meant to be head games, it's just our way of trying to maintain some control, even while our hearts flutter wildly in being with our man."

Chase nodded. "Now that you mention it, I suppose Rochelle was like that, too."

"Exactly. So why should Paula be any different?" Monica asked. "Women are women. We just want to be appreciated and pursued, even if the man's already captured us."

Chase frowned. "The problem is, I'm not quite sure we're there yet insofar as knowing who's hooked whom."

"I think it's a mutual thing," she said over her mug. "Give Paula a little more time, and I'm sure she will happily accept your invitation."

Chase chuckled. "Maybe you should write a book on all this stuff. It would probably be a bestseller."

"Yeah, right," Monica scoffed. "Once I've retired from the diamond business, I'll have the time for that."

"Not much chance that will happen," he said. "Something tells me we're both in this business for the long haul."

"Probably." Monica eyed him. "Just relax with Paula and don't push her too hard. Some women tend to back off if they feel too pressured."

Chase drew his brows together. "You're saying I shouldn't have asked Paula to go to Antwerp?"

"Not at all," insisted Monica. "That was the right thing to do. In fact, she probably would've been hurt if you hadn't."

"But I don't want Paula to feel under any pressure to do what she's not comfortable doing. That's not me."

"I know that, and so does she. I also know that you're a lonely widower trying to find love again. Maybe you've found it with Paula. I just don't want you to blow it by overreaching." Monica leaned forward. "You're doing fine giving it your best effort. Just go with the flow and don't worry so much. It will all work out."

"I hear what you're saying," Chase told her, feeling better about the situation.

"Do you?" Monica looked skeptical.

He grinned, appreciating her shoulder to lean on. "Yes, loud and clear. I promise not to seem too desperate or pushy. I like Paula and respect her as a lady who is her own person and happens to make me happy. Whether she goes to Antwerp or not, we definitely seem to be headed for bigger and better things."

"I agree," Monica said. "There's no telling how far you two might go, if you allow it to happen."

Chase started at the thought. He realized it was totally in his character to have a woman like Paula in his life. He hadn't known until recently just how much he missed a strong intimate connection. There was no going back for him now, and if things went his way, Paula would echo these sentiments.

"Chase is taking you to Antwerp?" Virginia's eyes widened as she sat across the table from Paula at a café.

"I haven't given him my answer yet, but yes," Paula said elatedly over a steaming latte. "It caught me totally off guard when he asked me."

"Aren't surprises what true romance is all about?"

"I suppose." Paula sipped her coffee. "I didn't realize that he goes there every year to buy diamonds."

"So now you've uncovered another layer of the man and his travels." Virginia nibbled on a glazed donut. "I am so jealous that you've met someone who's clearly prepared to go the extra mile for you, no pun intended."

Paula smiled. "I think we're both committed to following our hearts. Then there's our physical attraction to each other."

"Oh, yes, you can't leave that out." Virginia chuckled. "Something tells me there will be plenty of time in Antwerp to work on the sex appeal."

"Chase will be there on business first and foremost," Paula reminded her. "Seems as if Antwerp is the place to go for those in the diamond trade. Chase will represent McCord Diamonds in purchasing diamonds and making contacts."

Virginia's eyelids fluttered. "And you think he's just bringing you along for the ride?"

"I didn't say that." Not exactly.

"Wake up, girlfriend. The man could've hopped on a plane all by his lonesome and resumed your torrid romance when he got back. Instead, Chase asked you to go with him. Doesn't that tell you something?"

Paula gazed at her. "Yes, that he would miss me like crazy," she avowed honestly.

Virginia tapped her hand. "Exactly!"

"It works both ways," Paula admitted dreamily. "So I guess that makes both of us a little crazy."

Virginia smiled. "I have a sneaky feeling that the *L* word might be spoken real soon."

Paula beamed at the notion. She would love to hear Chase say that he loved her, but she didn't want to get her hopes up. Maybe it was too soon for them to know what they felt on that level. Or perhaps the feelings were just one-sided when it came to the ultimate emotional commitment.

"Let's just wait to see how it goes," Paula uttered, seeking to downplay her expectations. "If and when the *L* word comes up, I'll deal with it."

Virginia's eyes widened. "What better place to exchange I love yous than when you're surrounded by glittering diamonds?"

Paula couldn't help but smile. "You really are the quintessential romantic."

"And you aren't?"

"Hope springs eternal," Paula said poetically, a fever of suspense building. "I think it's best not to speculate too much. Right now, I just need to let Chase know I'm going to Antwerp with him."

"Yes, you do. And make it snappy," Virginia said. "Tonight we've got some shopping to do."

"We do?"

"Of course. You have to dress for the part."

Paula smiled. "That's true."

"And undress, too." Virginia giggled.

Paula laughed. "You're so bad."

"Hey, I'm just being real," Virginia replied. "Let's face it—you'll be spending a lot time in bed, so you might as well make sure it's a memorable experience."

Paula's eyes twinkled. "I think that's pretty much a given." She thought about her previous sexual escapades with Chase that had left her panting and wanting more.

"I'm sure you're right about that," Virginia agreed.

Paula sipped her latte. "By the way, did you ever talk to Sheldon?"

"As a matter of fact, I did," Virginia said. "You won't have to worry about him coming around anymore trying to cause trouble."

"Are you sure about that?" Paula asked, mindful of her latest encounter with him.

Virginia met her eyes. "Why? Do you know something I don't?"

"Yes." She told Virginia about him showing up in the park this morning. "Maybe he didn't get the message."

"That's true. Or maybe you guys just happened to be at the same park at the same time."

Paula frowned. "You really believe that?"

Virginia sighed. "I'll talk to Sheldon again."

"Don't," Paula said. "I don't want to drag this out any further. I think I finally got through to him. To be on the safe side, I'll pick a different place to do my running, so there are no more so-called coincidences."

"That's probably a good idea. Overall, I believe Sheldon knows that he crossed the line with his behavior and that playing the wronged ex-lover was getting him nowhere fast."

"Yeah, we'll see if that holds up," Paula said guardedly.

"Supposedly he's got his eye on someone else now," Virginia remarked.

"He mentioned something to that effect. I hope the new lady knows what she's getting herself into."

Virginia sat back. "We all make mistakes and, hopefully, learn from them."

Paula nodded. "I know I've certainly made my fair share in the past. And Sheldon was one of them."

"That's history. You're living in the present now and looking toward a future that couldn't be brighter. Chase is clearly a few cuts above every other man you've dated."

"So very true," Paula agreed. "I don't know how I managed to get so lucky."

"Luck had absolutely nothing to do with it," Virginia told her flatly. "You're just getting what you've always deserved from a guy—someone who worships the ground you walk on and is secure enough not to smother you in the process. And if you play your cards right, that feeling just might last a lifetime."

The thought of spending her life with Chase agreed with Paula. She could easily imagine being with Chase till they were white-haired, in rocking chairs, living on memories and their unending love. However, she wasn't about to make the mistake of jumping the gun. It was best to take the days and nights as they came, and the rest would surely fall into place.

Chapter 16

Paula entered the offices of McCord Diamonds. She was immediately taken by the terra-cotta tiles and marble pillars, but wasn't as impressed with the perfunctory furniture in the lobby area. She envisioned what she could do with this space if the opportunity presented itself.

"Can I help you?"

Paula regarded the young woman at the reception desk. "I'm here to see Mr. McCord."

"Do you have an appointment?" she asked.

Paula frowned. "I'm afraid not, but I think he'll see me." She'd decided to surprise Chase, but now wondered if she should have phoned ahead.

"Your name?"

"Paula Devine."

"Just a moment please."

Paula listened as the receptionist announced her. She was excited to tell Chase that she would happily accompany him to Belgium and hoped it would be the beginning of many trips they would take to interesting places around the world.

"Mr. McCord will be right with you," the receptionist told her. "Feel free to have a seat if you like."

Paula opted to stand, feeling slightly nervous as she leaped into a whole new phase of their relationship.

"Well, hello…." The words came from behind her.

Paula recognized the deep voice as not belonging to Chase, but his father. She turned around and saw the elder Mr. McCord, grinning and looking dapper in a dark designer suit.

"Hi," she said.

His head tilted with amusement. "Something tells me you're looking for my son, not me."

Paula smiled, embarrassed that she hadn't asked for Chase by his first name. She'd practically forgotten that he shared the surname with his father. "Yes, I am. Sorry if I brought you out here for nothing."

Sylvester chuckled. "No apologies necessary. You're not the first person to get one McCord instead of the other. I needed a break anyway. It's good to see you again, Paula."

"You, too."

Sylvester favored the receptionist. "Celeste, Ms. Devine is a personal friend of Chase's."

"Oh." The receptionist studied Paula. "Would you like me to ring him?"

"That won't be necessary," Sylvester said. "I'll take her to his office." He paused. "Paula might need your help with something later, though."

Celeste nodded. "Okay, I'll be here."

Paula smiled at her and wondered what help she might need. She followed Sylvester out of the lobby and past a window display of glistening diamonds and other beautiful gemstones. Several abstract paintings were hung on the opposite wall.

"You did a wonderful job with Chase's house," Sylvester told Paula.

"I'm glad you think so," Paula said graciously. "I just added to the beauty that was already there."

"Indeed you did." Sylvester grinned. "I understand you might be working your magic around here, too?"

"I'd love to take a look about and offer my recommendations for redecorating."

"I'm sure Chase will be happy to hear your ideas on upgrading the place, and you have my full backing. Celeste can assist you."

"Thanks for the vote of confidence," Paula said sincerely.

Sylvester's eyes crinkled. "You've earned it. Chase and I are satisfied customers," he said. "By the way, you've done so much more for my son than redecorate rooms in his house. You've given Chase new life again. I'm seeing a side of him that all but disappeared when he lost his wife."

Paula was touched by his words. "He's given me at least as much to cherish," she replied. "Chase is a wonderful guy, and it's been great getting close to him."

Sylvester smiled broadly. "I wish you both the best."

She batted her eyes and, again, was not sure how to respond. It had never occurred to Paula that Chase's father could be just as enthusiastic as her grandmother in wanting their relationship to work.

Chase sat at his desk, working and daydreaming about Paula, as had become a habit of late, when he heard the office door open. He saw his father enter and then Paula, causing Chase's heart to skip a beat.

"Look who popped in," Sylvester said in a bubbly voice. "I thought I'd stretch these old legs a bit and walk Paula to your office."

Chase sprung to his feet happily. "Thanks, Dad."

"I was happy to do it." Sylvester patted him on the shoulder. "I'll leave you two alone now. Oh, don't forget we've got a meeting at five, Chase."

Chase nodded, knowing they needed to discuss sales and possible expansion. "I'll see you then."

Sylvester eyed Paula. "Thanksgiving is coming up soon. If you don't have any other plans, my wife and I would like you and Chase to have dinner with us."

"I'd love to." She looked at Chase. "Unless you had something else in mind?"

He smiled, thinking of them in bed together. That would come later. "No, it sounds fine to me."

"Then it's settled." Sylvester's eyes creased at the corners. "I'll let Evelyn know."

Chase waited till his father left before pulling Paula close to him. "Looks like we've got ourselves a dinner date for Thanksgiving," he said enthusiastically. "Turkey with all the trimmings."

"Your father can be very persuasive." Paula lifted her eyes. "Just like his son."

"Must be in the genes." Chase grinned slyly. "Or maybe it's the woman."

"Always a charmer," she teased.

"With you, I can't help myself."

She gave him a toothy smile. "I wouldn't want you any other way."

"I feel the same about you." Chase kissed Paula, allowing the kiss to linger while enjoying her tasty lips.

"That was nice," she murmured, licking her lower lip.

"Yes, it was." Chase met her gaze. "I didn't expect to see you here. It was a nice surprise."

Paula batted her lashes. "Wasn't I invited to come and assess the place for redecorating?"

He cracked a smile. "Of course."

"So here I am."

"I'm glad you came," he assured her.

Paula paused. "I admit that I had an ulterior motive."

Chase cocked a brow. "Is that so?"

She pressed her open mouth to his for a long moment. "Yes."

Chase took in her kiss while thinking about his invitation

to Antwerp. He hoped she would accompany him so they could turn it into a new place to explore their romance.

Paula ran her pinky across his lips. "About your trip to Belgium…"

He tensed. "Yes?"

She smiled. "Count me in. There's nothing I'd like more than to go off to a faraway land of romance and diamonds with you."

Chase beamed. "I'm so happy to hear that. I promise we'll have a great time."

"That's a given," she tossed at him. "Whenever we're together, it feels perfect."

He pulled their bodies close again. "I couldn't agree more. Now you see why I'm finding it hard to let you out of my sight and away from my arms."

"Hmm…" Paula kissed him, wrapping her arms around his neck. "I seem to be developing that same affliction."

Chase slipped his tongue in her mouth. "Maybe it's incurable."

"Maybe it is," she cooed, giving him several quick kisses. "I guess some things you just have to live with."

"You won't get any complaints from me," he promised, peppering her face with quick kisses. "Not one."

Paula swallowed. "It's getting kind of hot in here."

"I hadn't noticed," Chase said softly as his temperature rose.

"Yeah, right." She moved her face just beyond his lips. "If it were up to you, we'd probably have sex right here in your office."

He peered lasciviously at her. "That's not a bad idea."

"What if someone comes in?" Paula asked nervously.

"That's what locks are for."

"But they might hear us," she said self-consciously.

"We'll keep the noise down, and I'll turn on my CD player," Chase said calmly. "That should let us do our thing without anyone else knowing."

Paula smiled. "You think of everything."

"I try."

Right now all Chase could think of was the ultrasexy woman before him. Seeing her naked beneath him on his desk would be a big turn-on, but he would settle for being deep inside her with those sexy, long legs wrapped around him.

Chase gave Paula a smooch. "Wait right here."

"I'm not going anywhere," she murmured.

He read the hunger in her eyes, mirroring his. "That's music to my ears."

Chase had all his calls held, and then, taking long, looping strides, he locked the door. It effectively shut them off from the rest of the world, so it was just the two of them, free to explore their passion with no distractions.

Paula watched as Chase loosened his tie and then unzipped his pants. His erection practically sprang out, arousing her with its throbbing size. She unbuttoned her blouse just to give him a hint of cleavage before lifting her skirt above her hips and pulling down her panties. She backed up to his desk and waited for him to slip on a condom.

Paula's mouth watered at the prospect of having Chase inside her. She'd never had sex in an office before and found it very exciting. Being with him, no matter where they were, made her senses come alive, and she was more open-minded than she ever thought possible. Chase really brought out the woman in her. She wanted to soar as high as she could, as long as he floated in the clouds beside her.

"You are so damn beautiful," Chase said gutturally, holding her cheeks.

"This beautiful lady is all yours," Paula cooed, surrendering to him. "Whatever you want, you've got."

His eyes danced. "You make me crazy."

Paula ran her tongue across her lips, feeling hot with desire, too. "It must be catching," she said, reaching out to touch Chase.

Chase angled his face and brought their mouths together. They kissed vehemently, caught up in their mutual attraction and desperate need. Neither backed away from the moment, determined to see it through.

Paula sucked Chase's lower lip, drawing it inside her mouth. She loved his taste and scent, feeling them become a part of her. She moved to his upper lip, sucking it while her tongue circled his at a frantic pace.

Chase slid his hand inside her blouse and began caressing Paula's taut nipples. She screamed silently as the sensations jolted her. He put his other hand beneath her skirt and found what he was looking for, gently stroking Paula's clitoris. With the ache between her legs growing steadily, Paula grabbed Chase's penis.

"Now, baby," she whispered insistently. "Don't make me wait for you any longer."

"I hear you," Chase groaned as he pressed his hands to Paula's waist and lifted her onto the desk. She opened her thighs, inviting him in. Chase moved forward, and she slid toward his erection, lowering herself on him. Paula wrapped her legs around his back, taking him fully inside, reveling in the intense pleasure.

Chase cupped her buttocks, bringing them closer together while thrusting deeper and deeper inside Paula. He hit the spot repeatedly with precision and determination. She resisted the urge to scream in case she alerted others, instead taking quick breaths and uttering tiny whimpers. Paula could feel Chase's heart pounding against her breasts as they clung together and went at each other frantically and with a sense of desperation.

When her orgasm neared, Paula clutched Chase's back and breathed erratically. She kissed his face uncontrollably and rubbed her clitoris against him as the buildup spread like fire throughout Paula. She shuddered violently while the powerful sensations overtook her whole body with incredible ecstasy. As if he had waited for her, Chase's body suddenly broke into spasms as his breathing quickened.

Paula absorbed his powerful trusts, relishing the feel of his manhood as their peaks of pleasure mounted simultaneously.

Chase conquered her mouth with blazing, soulful kisses, which she returned in earnest, gnawing at his lips fervently. When it was over and their equilibrium had returned to near normal, they broke out into unabashed laughter like children.

"Welcome to McCord Diamonds," Chase said jovially, discarding the condom and fastening his pants.

Paula buttoned her blouse. "That was quite a welcome. You sure do know how to make a girl feel right at home, Mr. McCord."

He chuckled. "It was my pleasure."

"Uh, I think at least half the pleasure was mine."

"I can accept that. Share and share alike," Chase said. "Things just keep getting better between us all the time."

"Yes, they do," she said softly. They did seem to be hitting on all cylinders in building a solid relationship. It made her believe that anything and everything was possible with such a wonderful man. "I guess it says something about us."

Chase gazed at her. "What might that be?"

"That we're the real deal!"

"Yeah, we sure are." He kissed Paula and then grinned broadly. "I can't wait to take you to Antwerp."

Her eyes sparkled. "It sounds very exciting."

"That's because of you," he said straightforwardly.

Paula blushed. "I think you put me on much too high a pedestal."

"I disagree. You're right where you belong. You're the whole package in one sexy-as-hell body, and I feel very fortunate to have you in my life."

"You're so sweet," she told him emotionally, "and a pretty special guy, too."

Chase looked at her tenderly. "Is that so?"

"It sure is. Having you as my guy just makes it all the more incredible."

"We are pretty amazing together," Chase acknowledged.

Paula gazed up at his eyes before turning to his incredibly desirable lips, wanting badly to kiss them again.

Chase answered her thoughts, bringing his mouth down to hers. She opened her lips and met his halfway. The kiss was dizzying and delicious.

A warm streak of desire ran through Paula. No one had ever made her feel so special.

Chapter 17

Paula looked out the airplane window from her seat in first class. She could only see clouds below, which seemed to epitomize where her head was these days. Chase had opened her mind to a whole new world of possibilities, and she treasured each and every moment they spent together, wanting to believe with all her heart that their journey had only just begun.

She broke out of her reverie when Chase nibbled on her ear.

"See anything interesting out there?" he asked.

Paula turned his way with a smile. "Not half as interesting as what's in here."

"I'll take that as a compliment." He flashed a cute grin. "So, are you ready to take Antwerp by storm?"

"Am I ever," she voiced with eagerness.

"Great." He leaned back. "There's a lot to see and do."

"I can't wait to immerse myself. I look forward to being on your arm in this exploration."

"I wouldn't have it any other way," Chase said and kissed Paula as if to seal the deal.

* * *

The five-star hotel was located in the center of the diamond district. They checked into a suite with a spectacular view of the city.

Chase came up behind Paula as she stood at the window and wrapped his arms around her waist. "So, what do you think?"

"It's beautiful."

He turned her around. "Just like you."

A bright smile lifted Paula's cheeks. "I can never get enough of hearing you say I'm beautiful."

"Glad you feel that way," he asserted, "since I plan to keep saying you're beautiful, because I mean it from the bottom of my heart."

Paula reached up and gave him a mouthwatering kiss that made Chase appreciate that he was a man. The fact that she was his woman and here with him in Antwerp made him believe life truly was looking up for both of them.

After freshening up, they went to the hotel's restaurant for dinner.

"How nice to see you again, Mr. McCord," said the maître d' as he took them to their seats.

"Nice to be back in Antwerp," Chase told him.

"The diamond business must be still very good in the States, yes?"

"Everyone likes diamonds," Chase said with a smile.

"Ahh, but of course." The maître d' flashed his teeth. "May I suggest you start off with a glass of Châteauneuf-du-Pape Château de la Gardine red wine?"

Chase eyed Paula. "That sounds fine."

"Very well," he said. "Enjoy your stay in Antwerp."

"Just how many times have you been to this hotel?" Paula asked curiously after the maître d' left.

Chase picked up his menu. "Actually, just one time. It was earlier this year."

"And he remembers you from then?"

"Well, as a gentleman jeweler of color with an American

accent who happens to leave big tips, it probably wasn't that much of a stretch to remember that I dined here some months earlier."

"I suppose." Paula studied her menu. "So, were you here alone, or should I just mind my own business?"

Chase grinned, not at all put off by her inquisitiveness. "It's a fair question. Yes, I was here alone for business. I haven't come with anyone since Rochelle died."

Paula flushed. "Oh, I'm sorry, Chase. I really didn't mean to sound jealous."

"It's okay. You have the right to be curious about my relationships," Chase said. He didn't want to keep anything from her. "I've gone out on dates over the past two years, mostly as a result of well-meaning friends who felt sorry for me being on my own. None of them amounted to anything. Then you came into my life…"

"I see." Her eyes batted. "And how much has that amounted to?"

"Everything," he told her evenly. "The more time we've spent together, the more time I want to spend with you."

Paula met his gaze warmly. "You really mean that, don't you?"

"Every word of it."

"Well, you're not alone in those feelings," she said, offering a warm smile.

"I was hoping you'd say that." Chase smiled back. "Now, what would you like to order?"

The following day, Chase took Paula to visit the famous Diamond Museum. Walking down the dark corridors containing brightly lit cases filled with diamond jewelry from the sixteenth century to the present, she felt as though she'd stepped back in time. Paula was awestruck at everything from regal diamond diadems and bravura tiaras to a replica of the British Crown Jewels.

"This is really amazing," Paula told Chase, holding his hand comfortably.

"Yes, it is. Diamonds are the wonder of the world."

This was something Paula could truly appreciate. Her grandmother's sad tale of lost love had left an indelible impression on Paula of the power of a diamond ring and the eternal bond between two people meant to be together in spirit forever.

Paula wanted more than anything to have that same deep bond. She sensed such might be possible with Chase. Though he had known this kind of great love once, she sincerely believed there was more than enough room in his heart to experience it again with her. Paula sucked in a deep breath, wanting to stay on an even keel, but finding it hard not to allow her imagination to run wild with romantic possibilities. If Chase were ever to propose to her, she couldn't imagine turning him down. Not when the feelings stirring within her were as real as any she had known and figured to get stronger over time.

"Let's go upstairs," Chase said enthusiastically. "You've got to see a diamond cutter at work. You'll also learn more about the production of diamonds. I think it's all quite fascinating."

"I have no doubt about that," Paula said, her interest piqued. Just as she didn't doubt Chase had proven to be every bit as fascinating as any diamond might be.

That afternoon, while Chase attended to business, Paula visited the Royal Academy of Fine Arts, one of Europe's most influential fashion academies. She enjoyed exploring the place that was the training ground for many of the world's finest clothing designers.

Later she went shopping on one of the city's pedestrian streets, featuring an eclectic assortment of posh boutiques and trendy stores. She bought a couple of nice dresses and a power business suit that Paula thought looked great. She eventually made her way to a cozy lingerie shop in search of a dazzling teddy. There Paula found the perfect hot-pink lace teddy. She couldn't wait to put it on for Chase.

She paid for her purchase and went back to the hotel. While glancing over the room-service menu for lunch, the phone rang.

"Hello, gorgeous," Chase's voice said smoothly.

"Did you miss me already?" she asked playfully.

"Absolutely! I was taking a break from the diamond marketplace and thought I'd check on you."

"That was thoughtful."

"Find anything in the stores to buy?" Chase asked.

Paula chuckled. "What woman doesn't go shopping and find things she likes?"

"Sorry I asked," Chase said with a laugh.

"I bought something for you, too," she told him.

"Is that so?"

"It is so."

"A bit early for Christmas gifts, isn't it?" asked Chase.

"It's never too early for those," Paula replied.

"Hmm, sounds intriguing. So what did you buy me?"

"I'm not going to tell you," Paula teased, "or it would spoil the surprise."

"I like surprises," Chase said in a sexy tone, "especially coming from you."

"See you soon," she told him with a little mystery in her voice.

"Count on it." Chase made a kissing sound. "Later."

She hung up and realized that she'd begun to depend on Chase more each day. Was that a good thing? Paula believed with all her heart that it was a very good thing.

Chase wondered what Paula had bought for him. He had a few ideas, but was content to wait and see. Just hearing her voice had given him a rise. The lady was definitely getting under his skin, and he was growing very comfortable with that.

Chase continued making the rounds amongst his representatives in the diamond district. He purchased a variety of excellent graded, clean, certified loose diamonds, along with diamond bands, bracelets and earrings with variations in color, clarity, cut and proportion. They would all be shipped to Silver Moon, processed, and sent to the stores accordingly. Acting as a broker for customers, Chase also filled a few orders for diamonds that included an official international "cut in Antwerp" label.

He was particularly interested in getting something very special for Paula on this trip, short of an engagement ring, but a strong indicator of how he felt about her. If things continued to move in the right direction, Chase felt there was every reason to believe that this could eventually lead to marriage. He wanted nothing more than to have the same loving, committed relationship that he had had with Rochelle. Paula seemed to fit the bill more perfectly with each passing day, unlike others he had dated who were not marriage material in his eyes. Chase sensed that she was someone who had the same strong convictions as he did in wanting to make a life of love and commitment with the right person. Paula was a lady whom he felt he could depend on through thick and thin, and Chase could easily picture himself showering her with endless affection and gifts to her heart and body's content.

Chase stood at the counter, studying a row of diamond pendants. All were eye-catching, yet only one seemed perfect for what he had in mind. It was a four-prong, platinum, heart-shaped pendant with white and chocolate diamonds totaling one carat.

"What do you think?" the clerk asked anxiously.

Chase pretended to contemplate it further before lifting up the heart-shaped pendant he wanted to surprise Paula with. The diamonds sparkled luminously.

"I believe I've found what I'm looking for," Chase said with satisfaction.

The clerk's face creased when he smiled. "Excellent choice. I'm sure the lady will melt when you put this around her neck."

"I think so, too." Chase imagined that he would take delight showering Paula with diamonds just as he once had Rochelle.

She had never failed to appreciate diamonds as an expression of his feelings for her. Chase felt certain that would also be the case with Paula, who had come into his life when he needed her most. Chase intended to do his part to make sure she was there to stay.

"What's this?" Paula blinked while looking at Chase's gift.

"It's a box of Belgium chocolates," he said. "I definitely couldn't let you leave here without trying some."

She smiled at the gesture. "Thank you. I love chocolate. Maybe even a little too much."

Chase gave her the once-over. "If that's true, I can't see it anywhere."

Her lashes fluttered. "And just what do you see?" she challenged.

"I see a lady who obviously takes very good care of herself."

Paula beamed. She was happy to hear that her hard work as a jogger and fitness buff had paid off. She eyed his tight physique, envisioning his body naked. "I could say the same thing about you."

"Thanks." He grinned. "I have something else for you, too."

"You do?" She met his gaze.

"Yes. Close your eyes."

Paula did as he asked, very curious as to what he might have up his sleeve. She felt him put something around her neck.

"Okay, you can open them now."

She opened her eyes and couldn't believe it when she saw the sparkling diamond pendant. "Oh, Chase…"

"You like it?"

Paula turned to him. "I love it. It's absolutely gorgeous!"

Chase's eyes crinkled. "A gorgeous diamond pendant for a gorgeous woman."

She held the pendant, mesmerized by the intensity of the chocolate and white diamonds, and lifted her face to look at Chase. "Thank you."

"I wanted you to have something truly memorable of our

visit to Antwerp," he said sweetly. "When I saw this, I knew it was made just for you."

Paula kissed him. "You're so good to me."

"We're good to each other and for each other," Chase said as he gazed into her eyes.

"I totally agree," she said, looking up at him.

"I was hoping you'd say that."

Chase wrapped his arms around Paula and kissed her lustfully. Their mouths stayed connected as she put her all into the kiss and the man behind it. Everything else seemed to be a blur, so focused was she in the moment at hand.

After several hot minutes of kissing, Chase separated their lips, but continued to hold Paula. "So how long are you going to keep me in suspense about what you bought for me?"

Paula licked her lips. "Not long at all. Why don't you get ready for bed, and I'll be right with you in a couple of minutes."

A wide smile played on Chase's lips. "I'm always up for getting naked to be with you."

"Me, too," Paula said shamelessly, though this time she had something else in mind for him.

She was aroused just thinking about his perfect nude body and his full erection aching to be deep inside of her. After another look at her diamond pendant, Paula was even more eager to pleasure her man.

Chase waited impatiently on the bed while Paula was in the bathroom. He was always incredibly turned on at the thought of making love to her. This time, doing so in another part of the world made it all the more erotic and thought provoking. Chase knew without a doubt that Paula was someone he simply would not ever tire of intimately. Did that mean real and sustainable love was not far behind? He wondered if she was asking herself the same question.

When Paula came out, the bathroom light shone on her hot-pink teddy. Embroidered with sequin and a black bow, it was very revealing, with a deep V neckline bordered by Chantilly lace. The satin fabric clung to every curve of her sexy body, while the thigh-high cut accentuated the length of Paula's legs.

"Here's your present," she said teasingly and turned all the way around to tempt him even more, showing in the process an erotic stretch-lace thong back. "I hope it meets with your approval?"

He salivated. "Oh, yes, I'm more than satisfied."

"I'll keep it on all the way through, or take it off when you want." Paula posed sinuously. "Better yet, I'll just leave that part up to you."

Chase grinned lustfully. He loved seeing and touching her naked body, but he also felt she looked sexy as hell in lingerie. "Right now, all I want is you, baby," he told her in a husky voice.

"Then you'll have me every way you can imagine," she uttered, "and maybe even a few ways beyond your wildest imagination."

"Hmm, I definitely like the sound of that," Chase murmured.

Paula grabbed a piece of chocolate and climbed atop Chase. She bit off half and then held the rest to his mouth. He took it in greedily. He'd begun to chew when she bent her face down, licked his lips and kissed him passionately. Chase reciprocated as the melting chocolate passed between them.

She lifted back up, arching her back, and began to stimulate his nipples adroitly with her fingertips. Chase shut his eyes and reveled in the pleasure. His hands reached inside the teddy and cupped her breasts, stroking and titillating them. Paula gasped when he squeezed her nipples and gently ran his fingernail over them.

She took hold of his engorged penis, fondling the length of him and playing with the tip. Chase bit his lip, fighting off the urge to come then and there, as he loved when they climaxed together.

Paula spun her body around so her back was to Chase. She lowered her face and went down on his erection. He trembled as her mouth covered him and her tongue teased expertly. With a salacious view of Paula's backside, Chase was eager to taste her sweet goodness. He held her buttocks and lifted his head, using his tongue to push past the teddy till he found Paula's clitoris. He licked and sucked and twirled his tongue while she moaned with pleasure, trembling wildly.

Soon Chase's mouth covered the entire area of Paula's genitalia, kissing and sucking even as she did the same to him in glorious sixty-nine. Once the oral copulation had resulted in mutual powerful orgasms, they rearranged themselves on the bed. Still hungry for more of his hot lover, Chase slipped on a condom and climbed on top of Paula.

He slid inside her, penetrating as far as she wanted him, thrusting mightily while she tightened around his erection. Her legs were splayed wide, and their slick bodies pressed together in harmonious movement. They kissed passionately, the scent of their sex intoxicating, raising the intensity of Chase's arousal to new heights.

"Go deeper," Paula urged him, lifting her legs off the bed. "Much deeper."

Driven by her words and his overpowering desire, Chase propelled himself forward in rapid motion, burrowing through the soft, moist walls of her sexuality. His penis conquered the depths within, bringing cries of exultation from Paula.

Chase moaned and quavered with his second climax, leaving him slightly light-headed. He continued to perform determinedly till Paula yielded to her pleasure, her contractions coming in waves. She huffed and puffed, digging her nails into the flesh of his lower back till settling down.

They kissed zealously as the perfect way to finish what their desire had started.

Chase and Paula spent the following day touring Brussels, the largest urban area in Belgium and the capital of the European Union. Paula enjoyed visiting Grand Place, the historic market square; Bruparck, a leisure and shopping center; the Belgian Comic Strip Center and the Basilica of the Sacred Heart church. At one point, they stopped at a street vendor, and Chase bought Paula a single long-stemmed red rose.

"A rose for a lovely lady," he said affectionately.

"Oh, how beautiful," Paula gushed.

Chase flashed his teeth. "Not half as lovely as you are."

Paula ate it up, feeling like she was the most fortunate woman in the world in being with the most desirable gentleman.

She kissed Chase on the mouth. They held hands as they continued to explore the city. Paula was sure this was all leading to something neither of them could control, and it was more powerful than anything she had ever experienced.

On their last day, they took a scenic candlelit-dinner cruise around the Antwerp harbor. Chase hand-fed Paula, and she did the same in return, finding the experience very romantic. They washed down the cuisine with goblets of sauvignon blanc.

Paula felt the heat of Chase's gaze. "What?" she asked, fearing she might have food on her face.

He maintained a serious look. "I'm falling in love with you."

Her heart skipped a beat. "Really?"

"Yes." Chase took her hand in his. "I hope that doesn't scare you, but this seemed like the perfect time and place to say it."

Paula was moved to hear the words, agreeing with him wholeheartedly that the moment could not have been more perfect. "It doesn't scare me at all," she assured him, meeting his eyes. "The truth is, I'm also falling in love with you." Paula spoke from her heart.

Chase grinned widely. "I was hoping you'd say that."

Her eyes grew wide. "How could I not develop such feelings, Mr. Everything?"

He chuckled. "That would make you Ms. Everything."

She glowed. "I can accept that coming from you."

"Then you can also accept this…."

Chase leaned over and kissed her tenderly on the lips. Paula could taste the wine on his mouth. She slid her tongue inside, gently probing till she found his tongue.

"Oh, yes, I can accept that anytime, anywhere," she assured him with affection.

Chase pulled back and looked at her longingly. "Consider it a kiss to build on."

"I'm looking forward to the building process." Paula puckered her lips, closed her eyes and eagerly dove back into the kiss.

Chapter 18

"Chase told me he was falling in love," Paula told Isabelle two days later as they had lunch at her grandmother's favorite restaurant.

Isabelle put her fork down. "I'm not surprised at all. What took him so long?"

Paula smiled. "I guess some men need longer than others to get in touch with their feelings," she joked. "Yes, I know it has been a whirlwind romance of less than two months. But some people click sooner than others."

"Don't I know it," Isabelle said over a cup of tea.

Paula looked across the table. "Exactly how long was it before Gramps uttered those magical words to you?"

"Oh, it took him only about four weeks to say he loved me." She chuckled. "He probably wanted to tell me after the first couple of dates but showed some restraint for fear of how I might respond."

Paula grinned while putting down her chicken sandwich.

"So you were confident he was being sincere and not just hoping to get lucky?"

Isabelle colored. "Oh, yes, he was definitely speaking from his heart. In those days, men couldn't count on 'luck' to get what they wanted. Certainly not from me, and with my daddy looking over both our shoulders."

Isabelle laughed, and Paula did the same. She knew that her circumstances were different from Isa's, as were the times. But the issue of love was every bit as serious and real. "I suppose, by comparison, Chase waited forever to say he loved me."

"What's important is that he said what was in his heart and put the onus on you to do the same," Isabelle said.

Paula sighed. "Actually, I wasn't sure I'd ever hear those words from someone who meant them."

"And why not?" Isabelle's eyes narrowed. "You're the type of woman any man in his right mind would fall for."

Paula took a bite from a pickle. "I don't know if I would be right for any man. With Chase, we get along great, have tremendous chemistry and are in sync romantically. I just wasn't sure if he would be able to get past the love he had for his late wife in order to be able to feel that way about another woman."

"Well, now you know that the man's living for today and not yesterday. It's you who has become the center of his world, and he wasn't afraid to spit it out."

Paula nodded. "I realize that now."

Isabelle crinkled her eyes. "The fact that Chase has given you the love you deserve makes me extremely happy."

"I'm happy, too," Paula assured her, trying not to get too emotional.

"So, I take it you also opened up with Chase and told him how you really feel?"

Paula beamed thoughtfully. "Yes, how could I not? I told him I was falling in love with him. I've known it for a while now, but didn't want to jump the gun before I knew how he felt."

"Makes sense," Isabelle said, forking a piece of lettuce from her salad. "Women always get there sooner than men.

I'm old-fashioned enough to believe it's best to wait for the man to tell the woman how he feels first. That way she can be sure her love isn't being wasted."

"It's not wasted at all in this case." Paula dabbed a napkin on her lips. "Chase McCord is definitely worth waiting for to hear the words. Oh, Isa, he's such a wonderful man. I honestly never thought I'd be so fortunate to meet someone like him."

"I felt the same way about your grandfather," Isabelle told her wistfully. "He was also a generous, loving man with a heart of gold. A true gentleman if I ever saw one, and very good-looking. If the truth be told, I probably fell in love with him from the moment I laid eyes on him."

Paula smiled, feeling the love Isa felt for him was still as strong as ever. It was that type of everlasting love she wanted to have. "I wish I'd gotten to know Gramps."

"So do I. He would've had you eating out of his hands, child. Or maybe it would have been the other way around."

"Probably both," Paula chuckled.

"I think you're right," Isabelle said, laughing. "You're so much like your grandfather."

Paula imagined that he was looking down on her and Isa, grateful for the time he had had with his beloved. Just as Paula felt about Chase in the short time she'd gotten to know him. She was sure things between them would only get better and better. She peeked at her pendant. The diamonds glistened. Was it a prelude to an engagement ring, followed by a wedding band?

Paula allowed her imagination to run wild. She wanted the ring, wedding and all the trimmings that came with being in love. Did Chase want this, too? Her instincts said yes. She needed only to allow nature to take its course and not believe anything or anyone could stand in their way.

Chase drove to work, his thoughts filled with memories of the trip to Antwerp with Paula. It had gone even better than his best dreams. The way she had responded told him that

Paula felt exactly the same about where they were and could go in their relationship.

Fifteen minutes later, Chase was sitting in his father's office to discuss business. But first he wanted to break the news about his feelings for Paula.

"I'm in love, Dad."

Sylvester took off his glasses. "You've finally come to terms with this?"

Chase nodded diffidently. "Yeah, I guess I have."

"Have you told Paula?"

"In Antwerp," he responded, visualizing the exact moment the words were uttered.

Sylvester's eyebrows rose. "What did she say?"

"She feels the same way," Chase replied.

Sylvester put a big smile on his face. He stood up and went around his desk to give Chase a hug. "Congratulations, son. I'm glad you two have given in to the power of love."

Chase flashed a grin. "Thanks, Dad. It sure feels like something that was meant to happen, maybe from day one."

"Maybe it was. You deserve to have someone in your life who can make you happy again."

"Happiness is something I feared might not come my way again after Rochelle died," Chase conceded. "But Paula walked into my life and showed me that I still had enough love left inside to give to someone else."

Sylvester's eyes crinkled. "My hat's off to Paula for making you want much more than you already have."

Chase mused. Thanks to Paula, he did want so much more now and felt there was no limit to what they might be able to achieve together. He didn't necessarily expect that they wouldn't run into some bumps along the road as two people coming from different places in their lives, but Chase saw no reason why they couldn't agree on most points to achieve romantic harmony.

"So, are you thinking about making this love official?" Sylvester asked, gazing down at him.

Chase stared at the question long and hard. "Yeah, maybe." He paused pensively. "But we need to let our love settle in. I don't want to rush it. Paula deserves some time to come to grips with this whole thing and where she wants to go with it."

"You're right." Sylvester patted him on the shoulder. "You're both young and should take all the time you need to get it right. I just want you to be sure you're not somehow holding on to the past at the expense of the present—or the future, for that matter."

"I'm not," Chase tried to reassure him. "I know Rochelle's gone and not coming back. I've really understood that from the beginning, but it took a while to deal with. I'm over that now. I want to be with Paula and make a good life together, and I believe she wants the same. I'd be honored to be her husband and the father of her children. All we need is the right moment to put it all in motion."

Sylvester's eyes creased. "Son, I think you've already done that. The rest, whenever it happens, will just be the icing on a very nice cake."

Chase smiled, not disagreeing. Paula was just the type of dessert he'd been waiting for to enter his world. If he had his way, she would be there to stay with a cherry on top.

"Here we are," Chase said, pulling his car into the brick driveway on Thanksgiving Day. "My home away from home."

Paula marveled at the Mediterranean-style mansion owned by Sylvester McCord as if seeing it for the first time. She could never have imagined that by virtue of going to work for Chase's father, she would meet the true love of her life. She still had to pinch herself to believe it was real.

"It's magnificent," Isabelle uttered from the backseat, echoing Paula's thoughts.

She looked at her grandmother. Chase had cleared it with Sylvester for Isa to come along for the Thanksgiving meal. As her only real family, Paula wanted her grandmother to share in the relationship and happiness that was building with Chase and those closest to him.

"Wait till you see the inside," Paula told Isabelle as they headed up the cobblestone walkway amidst a dusting of snow.

"I'm sure it'll be just as nice."

"That's especially true for the recreation room," Chase said with a grin. "Thanks to your granddaughter's incredible talents."

"Oh, stop it." Paula hit him playfully. She never tired of the compliments, but still wanted to keep them in check so she didn't get too full of herself.

They were greeted warmly by Sylvester and Evelyn.

"Welcome to our home," Evelyn said after being introduced to Isabelle in the spacious living room.

"Thank you for having me," Isabelle responded.

Sylvester smiled at her. "It's our pleasure. And now that Paula is practically family, that means you are, too."

Paula felt maudlin hearing his words. The fact that Chase's father and stepmother had accepted her as his girlfriend so graciously really meant a lot, especially since they had been the in-laws to Chase's late wife and now had to adjust to someone new in his life.

"I appreciate that," Isabelle said kindly. "Family has always been very important to me."

"I understand you're from South Africa?" Sylvester regarded her.

"Yes, Johannesburg."

"And when did you come to America?"

"I moved here with my parents when I was seventeen," Isabelle told him.

Sylvester touched his face. "So you've been here for a while."

She smiled. "More than half a century, I'm happy to reveal. I love living in the United States but will always consider South Africa home."

"Quite understandable," Sylvester told her. "I've traveled to the Northern Cape a few times for business. Beautiful country."

Isabelle's eyes lit. "That's what most people say. We South Africans are proud of the richness of our land and culture."

Having visited her ancestral homeland twice, Paula could attest to that. She'd gotten to see the village where her grandmother was born and experience the joys of unmatched hospitality. She hoped to go there again someday with Chase.

"Isabelle, why don't I give you and Paula a tour of the place, and then we'll have dinner?" Evelyn suggested.

"That sounds wonderful," she said.

Paula agreed. She was eager to see the parts of the fabulous multilevel house that she had missed during her last visit. She looked up at Chase. "See you in a bit."

He gave her a little hug and a smile. "Have fun."

An hour later they were seated in the formal dining room. The table was filled with platters of turkey, cornbread dressing, ham, greens, muffins and other food that Evelyn had made herself.

"This is absolutely delicious," Paula told her, tasting some dressing.

"Thank you," she said. "I do my best to try to keep two men with healthy appetites happy at the table."

Chase grinned, biting into a muffin. "You do a great job at it." He turned to Isabelle. "The same is true for Isa. If we play our cards right, Paula and I may never need to cook again."

Isabelle laughed. "That would be fine by me, as long as you do the dishes afterward."

Evelyn showed her teeth. "Isa and I definitely think alike."

"We certainly do," Isabelle agreed.

"It's all part of our conspiratorial game plan," Chase said with a wink. "Isn't that right, Paula?"

She smiled brightly, feeling the genuine warmth of his eyes. "Totally. But I still want to at least occasionally cook for you, honey," she told him.

"Anytime you want," he promised.

"It's also nice to dine at restaurants sometimes," Paula added. "That way neither of us has to worry about dirty dishes."

Chase chuckled. "Of course. See, Dad, we're already acting like an old married couple, minus the piece of paper."

Sylvester threw his head back with laughter. "You two are clearly enjoying each other's company. It's going to be wonderful to have you here over the Christmas holiday, brightening up our lives."

"That works both ways," Paula said, planning to invite him and Evelyn to her house before the year was through, especially now that Isa and Evelyn seemed to be on the verge of becoming good friends. Paula felt that things were definitely looking up in all areas as her relationship with Chase began to connect both of their families.

"I hope you're having a good time," Chase said, his arms wrapped around Paula's waist from behind.

"I'm having a great time." She looked at him over her shoulder, glad to have some time alone. "So is Isa."

"She told you that?"

"Didn't have to," Paula said perceptively. "Isn't it obvious that your father and stepmother have been very gracious hosts? Anyone would feel right at home with them."

"Yeah, I suppose so." Chase's mouth curved upward. "Guess I'm used to them being the amazing people they are."

Paula smiled. "You're definitely cut from the same cloth."

"Think so, huh?"

"If I didn't, I wouldn't be so crazy about you," she admitted.

Chase turned her around. "Hmm, maybe later I can play doctor and work on that affliction?"

Paula batted her eyes teasingly. "Sure you're up to the task?"

He pretended to consider it. "We'll just have to find out, but here's a clue...."

Chase held her cheeks and gave Paula a long, sensual, deep kiss, causing her knees to buckle.

"I don't mean to interrupt you two lovebirds," Sylvester said as he entered the room.

Pulling away from Chase, Paula saw Sylvester standing there, looking amused. "Oh, hi," she said, feeling embarrassed.

"Dad." Chase followed suit, standing up straight.

"Actually, I was hoping I could borrow your lady for a minute," he told Chase, then looked at Paula. "I wanted to catch you while you're here to take a look at the patio as a possible future project to tackle."

Paula eyed Chase, not wanting him to think she put business ahead of their pleasure. Not in this lifetime.

"Go right ahead," he said nonchalantly. "Just find me when you're done."

She touched her mouth that still tingled from his kiss. "Will do."

Paula trailed Sylvester through the house and across a parquet floor. She stepped onto the rotund concrete patio with stone columns and metal furniture.

"We added this furniture a few years ago," Sylvester said. "But Evelyn thinks it's time to replace it. Any ideas?"

Put on the spot, Paula was able to make a quick assessment. "Let's see," she said, looking around the room. "I can see you with some solid wood or teak furniture over here and maybe an umbrella table and chaise over there. Also, I think a fountain would be a terrific addition."

"That all sounds good. Why don't you draft a plan, and we'll run it by Evelyn? If she approves, we can schedule the work for early next year and hope the weather cooperates."

Paula smiled. "That's fine, and thank you." She felt privileged that he was giving her repeat business.

"I want to thank you for making my son smile again," Sylvester said in return. "It hasn't been easy for him since his wife died."

"I know," Paula said sadly.

"But things are much better for him now."

She met his eyes. "I think Chase and I owe much of that to you. If you hadn't brought us together…"

"I was happy to send Chase your way," Sylvester told her. "You both seemed like a match in the making, and I'm glad it worked out that way."

Paula's eyes welled with tears. "So am I."

"Be good to Chase and he'll be good to you," Sylvester said knowingly.

"I will," she promised.

"There you are," Isabelle said to Chase as he stood by the window, watching snowflakes fall.

"Isa."

He looked at her, seeing Paula as she might look in forty years. Chase was warmed by the notion that Paula's beauty and grace would hold up as well as Isabelle's had over the years.

"Thank you for making my ring seem like new again." Isabelle held up the hand with her gleaming wedding band. "I love it!"

Chase recalled earlier in the day when he and Paula had presented the ring to Isa. "It looks like it did fifty years ago," he'd bragged and placed on her finger.

"Actually better," Isabelle said, marveling. "If only my Earl could be here now to see this."

"I have a feeling he is with you at this very moment," Paula told her affectionately.

Isabelle became teary-eyed. "Yes, I know he's looking down on us all." She flexed her ring finger with pride and then gave Paula a big hug and Chase a bigger one.

He choked up now at the memory, especially in watching Isa take such joy in this symbol of her relationship with her beloved husband, Earl.

Chase smiled tenderly. "I was more than happy to restore the ring to its luster," he told her. "I know this ring means a great deal to you, as it should."

"Yes, it's like a window into the past for me," Isabelle said. "Because of it, my darling Earl is forever close to my heart. Until I see him in heaven, his gift of a lifetime is what keeps me going. Along with my remarkable granddaughter."

"Yes, she is certainly a remarkable lady," Chase agreed. "And so are you, Isa."

She beamed. "That's so sweet of you to say. It's easy to see how Paula fell in love with you."

He lifted a brow, pleased Paula had shared her feelings with Isabelle. "Thank you for the compliment. I assure you the feelings are mutual."

"I can see that. You two really seem to be meant for each other," Isabelle said sincerely.

Chase smiled thoughtfully. "I'd have to agree with you there."

Isabelle reached into her purse and removed what looked to Chase to be an old diamond ring.

"What's this?" he asked.

"It's my engagement ring. Earl gave it to me on Christmas many years ago," she told him. "I kept it tucked away, waiting for the day I could pass it to the man who stole Paula's heart."

Chase was nearly speechless. The idea that she would part with something obviously so precious and meaningful to her was incredible and maybe too much of a sacrifice for him to accept.

"I really appreciate the kind gesture," he said. "But I can't take your—"

"You're not taking it," Isabelle broke in swiftly. "I want you to have the ring."

Chase's brow creased. "Paula and I haven't gotten to the point yet where we've talked about marriage…."

"I understand." She patted his hand. "I would never presume to know your intentions toward my granddaughter and do not mean to try and pressure you into asking Paula to marry you if this wasn't what you had in mind down the line. But should it be your decision someday, it would mean so much to me if Paula inherited my engagement ring to begin her love for a lifetime. I know the ring needs to be refitted and cleaned. You can even feel free to add diamonds or do whatever you wish to put your imprint on it. I just felt this was the right thing to do and hope it doesn't put you off in any way."

Chase found his resistance waning. The love Isa felt for Paula was incredibly touching and rivaled his. How could he reject what seemed such a natural passing of the torch to

Paula? It was a gift that Paula richly deserved from the woman who meant so much to her. Isabelle had displayed selflessness that most people would never come close to.

He took the ring. Studying it briefly, Chase saw that it lacked a center stone. This was something that could easily be rectified. He would add a few other small things to give the ring new life and would present it to Paula when the time was right.

Chase regarded Isabelle. "No, it doesn't put me off." His lips spread into a smile. "I'll hold on to this ring, and I promise to take good care of it."

Isabelle wiped away tears. "I can't tell you how happy that makes me."

"I think you already have," Chase said, trying to keep his emotions in check. "Paula is very fortunate to have someone like you who cares so much about her." He was moved to hug Isabelle. "Thank you for raising such a wonderful woman and for your willingness to entrust me with your ring. I'll try not to let you down."

Isabelle's arms went around his waist. "I'm sure you won't, but it's much more important that you and Paula try not to let each other down. So long as you go with your hearts, there's no mountain you can't climb."

He smiled and put his arm across her shoulder. "Why don't we go see if we can find your granddaughter and everyone else?"

Isabelle looked up at him. "That's a good idea."

Chapter 19

Paula supervised while her crew removed the old furnishings and installed the new ones in Chase's den. Chase was donating his used furniture to those less fortunate, which her crew would take care of. She was pleased to be redecorating another room in his house, reminding Paula that she was still an interior decorator and Chase a client. It was important that her work always be taken as seriously as Paula took every person who hired her, even if Chase had come to mean so much to her beyond home refurbishing.

Paula cherished the romantic relationship she had forged with Chase, making all previous boyfriends fall well short of his total being and the way he made her feel. She had once thought true love might forever escape her, as if she didn't deserve to experience such. Now she knew nothing could be further from the truth. She'd fallen in love with a wonderful guy and received his love in return.

There was no engagement ring yet, but Paula refused to be bothered by it. The diamond pendant he'd given her, along with his heart, were more than enough at the moment. Whenever Chase was ready to offer more, she would be ready to accept it unwaveringly.

"Well, how are we looking in here?" She heard Chase's smooth voice as he entered the room.

Paula's eyes twinkled at him. "See for yourself."

As it was, she was just about to go find him in his home office—the spot where they had last shared a very long, delicious kiss. The workers had cleared out, as Paula was confident the job would pass the test of Chase's scrutiny. If not, they were just a cell-phone call away for rearranging things any way he wished.

She felt a knot in her stomach as Chase seemed to take an inordinately long time perusing his revamped den. He finally looked at her, a half smile forming on his lips.

"You're three for three," he declared. "Another job well done!"

Paula batted her lashes as if annoyed. "It sure took you long enough to answer. I was beginning to wonder if you were less than satisfied."

Chase laughed. "I had to keep you in suspense a little just to keep things lively."

She hit him playfully. "There are other ways to be lively."

"Don't I know it," he said in an erotic tone of voice.

"I'll bet you do." Paula imagined them burning up the sheets.

Chase pulled her up to him. "You smell good."

Paula raised her chin. "It's a new fragrance."

"It's very nice."

"Do you want to do something about it?" she challenged.

"I thought you had another appointment to go to?" Chase cocked a brow.

"I can cancel it if you want." Had she really become so audacious in their relationship? Paula answered her own question, knowing that Chase had definitely taken her libido to a whole new level, one that she was happy to share with him. She called and cancelled her appointment, never taking her eyes off Chase.

"Oh, yes, I like," he said, peering at her seductively.

She batted her eyes. "Why am I not surprised?"

"Because you know me too well." Chase grinned. "Or is it more that I know you?"

"Probably both," she admitted, quickly becoming aroused.

"Yeah, I agree." Chase kissed her passionately. "Now, about us doing something…"

Paula met his eyes. "Right here?"

He grinned mischievously. "It's very tempting, to say the least, especially with all the trouble you've gone through to make it so welcoming. But I think I'd like to take you to bed, literally."

Paula felt a warm stirring between her legs. "So why are we still talking about it?"

Chase's eyes clouded with desire. "Yes, why are we?"

He kissed her mouth succulently, and all else ceased to exist as far as Paula was concerned, other than a powerful need to be with Chase in the most intimate way.

After they were naked, the kissing resumed in bed. Paula kissed Chase everywhere, and he did the same, leaving goose bumps in the wake of his potent and determined lips. The exhilarating foreplay reached a blazing peak and brought Paula to the brink of climaxing.

Though she loved the feel of Chase's tongue on her clitoris and the sounds he made while licking her, she wanted desperately to come while his penis was lodged inside her. As such, she lifted his face up. "Make love to me now, baby."

He licked his lips and looked at her ravenously. "Say no more…."

After slipping on a condom, Chase propped Paula's legs on his shoulders. He drove his erection deep into her, and she easily adjusted to him, making for a perfect fit as their sex moved into high gear. Their mouths nibbled at one another's before their bodies locked in an intense embrace. Paula tasted the deliciousness of Chase's tongue and delighted in his manly scent.

She arched her body, taking him in all the way, her buttocks slamming against his hard stomach with each of Chase's thrusts. Their perspiring bodies clung together while their sizzling passion continued to soar. A low moan grew steadily from Paula as she felt the waves of orgasmic ecstasy building to a fever pitch. She wrapped her arms around Chase and trembled mightily when her climax took control of her mind and body. Grunting unevenly, Chase penetrated Paula deeper while his orgasm erupted. She gasped from the intensity of the moment and then rode the fervent rapids with him while they achieved rapturous victory together.

An hour later, Paula woke up in Chase's arms. The distinct smell of steamy sex was in the air, infiltrating her nostrils and arousing her once again. The man had turned her into a sex addict, and she didn't mind one bit. On the contrary, Chase had given Paula great incentive to want to make love to him as often as possible, for he was just as voracious in his appetite for her. They made an incredible match sexually, and when combined with their physical and mental chemistry, it was definitely an unbeatable combination.

Paula sighed deeply, and her cheeks rose as she smiled. She longed for the day when Chase would make her his wife. It would easily be the happiest day of her life, and she would make sure it was the happiest of his, too. She rested her head against his chest and allowed herself a bit more shut-eye and pleasant dreams.

The next day, Chase dragged the seven-foot white-spruce Christmas tree into the great room, eager to see it up and decorated. There hadn't been a tree in the house since Rochelle died, and he'd seriously wondered if that would ever change. Then Paula had come into the picture and made life worth living again. Moreover, between her decorating talents and her skills in the bedroom, she had brought magic back into the house in a big way.

"What do you think?" he asked Jackie.

"It's really big," she said, looking up at it.

He smiled. "Sure is, and it's a perfect fit for this corner, don't you think?"

"I suppose."

Chase lifted a brow. "You think I should've gotten an artificial tree?" It occurred to him that once the needles began to fall off, it would be her job to clean them up.

"I like this one." Jackie glanced at him. "But I'm not the one you should be asking."

"Oh?"

"You should ask Paula," Jackie said. "I'm sure she'll agree the tree fits the room perfectly."

He grinned. "I intend to put Paula to work helping me decorate it."

"Good luck with that," Jackie said lightheartedly. "And speaking of work, I better get back to it." She held up her dust rag for effect.

Chase nodded. "By the way, I'm sure I haven't told you this often enough, but I appreciate that you do such a great job keeping this place from falling apart."

Jackie flushed. "Thank you. I'm happy to do my job as long as you need me."

He expected he would need her for quite a while, though Chase hoped that before long Paula would move in with him as his wife. Then they could decide together what was needed in terms of housekeeping.

Paula sang along with Donny Hathaway as he crooned his hit song "This Christmas." She was helping Chase put ornaments on the Christmas tree, delighted to be able to share this age-old tradition with him. She hoped it would be the first of many holidays they would spend together. Maybe one day down the line there would also be some little ones to join in the celebration, she thought gleefully.

Chase wrapped his arms around her from behind. "You're just what I needed. A beautiful woman to help decorate the tree," he murmured, turning her around to face him.

Paula warmed at the thought, suspecting that hadn't been the case since his wife died. Could it also mean that soon she might become the next, and hopefully last, Mrs. Chase McCord?

"It's good to know you think I have the magic touch," she said warmly.

"You certainly do." He looked into her eyes. "And the magic kiss, too."

Paula opened her mouth to his waiting lips. She closed her eyes while they kissed, for a moment forgetting all about the decorating they had yet to finish. She reluctantly pulled her lips from his and playfully pushed him away. "If we don't get this tree done now, it might take us all night."

Chase laughed. "Don't give me any ideas."

"I think you already have enough ideas in that head of yours for both of us," she told him softly. Paula picked up an ornament and hooked it on the tree.

"Now that you mention it, I do have a great idea," he said mysteriously.

Paula looked at him expectantly. "And what might that be? Or shouldn't I ask?"

"It's not what you think, though that's certainly on the agenda." Chase added a few candy canes to the tree. "Now that you've completed the redecorating projects in my house, I'd like to give a holiday party to celebrate the season and show off the rooms."

"That's a great idea!" Paula said excitedly.

Chase looked at her. "I want it to be something we host together."

"Really?"

"Yeah. Invite whoever you want. It'll be a great chance for everyone to see what a fabulous couple we make."

"Oh, Chase." Paula got emotional. "How did you ever get to be so sweet and thoughtful?"

"Maybe you just bring out the best in me," Chase said warmly as he returned to decorating the tree.

Her lashes fluttered thoughtfully. "I could say the same about you."

He grinned. "Does that include your naughty side?"

"I'll leave that to your own active imagination," she said seductively.

Chase chuckled. "Okay, but just for now." He leaned over and kissed her. "Later, we'll see what my mind conjures up."

Paula licked her lips invitingly. "Whatever you say."

Twenty minutes later, the Christmas tree was finished. Paula stood back and marveled at the magnificent tree as the lights flashed on and off at different intervals. It reminded her of the Christmas trees from her childhood. In recent years, she'd gone with a small artificial tree that was easier to manage.

Chase put his arm across her shoulders, and Paula tucked her arm around his waist. Sharing the holiday season with the man she loved was more than she could have hoped for.

Chapter 20

"Thanks for meeting with me," Paula told Monica as they sat in the bistro.

"I'm glad you invited me. I needed a break from work, romance, drama, you name it," Monica said.

Paula chuckled. "Sounds serious…or not?"

Monica laughed. "Not. My life is all about such issues, and I suppose I can't really complain." She lifted her double espresso. "So, what's up with you?"

Paula paused while sipping on an Americano. "Well, with Christmas right around the corner, I'm in search of the perfect gift for Chase. I'm not sure what to give a man who seems to have everything."

"I see your dilemma," Monica said, sipping her coffee.

"Since you've known him for a long time, I was hoping you could suggest something."

Monica tilted her head. "I'm flattered that you reached out for my help. I'm not sure what to tell you as far as something to gift wrap. As for the *perfect* gift for Chase, I'm looking at her."

Paula blinked with surprise. "Seriously?"

"I'm being totally serious," she told her with a straight face. "It's been a long time since I've seen Chase so happy, flashing his million-watt smile constantly. And it's all because of you."

Paula allowed Monica's words to sink in. "Well, I'm sure he was that way when his wife was alive," she said, knowing the type of man Chase was.

Monica nodded. "I'm not going to lie to you. Chase and Rochelle had a really good relationship. I was sorry to see her pass so soon in life, but unfortunately these things happen. I'm glad Chase has moved on now."

"Thank you for that." Paula spoke sincerely. "I really want to make him the happiest man around."

Monica smiled. "I don't think you have to worry about that. Trust me, he's very happy."

Paula chose to trust herself more. She knew everything that bound her to Chase was very real, and having it validated by others made her confidence in their connection that much stronger. "I'm glad to hear that." She grinned demurely. "I'd still love to get Chase something for Christmas that speaks to him in a way he can truly appreciate."

Monica paused to think about it. "Hmm, since I know Chase is a gadget man, you might consider getting him a palm-size DVD player or a shirt-pocket HD camcorder."

"Interesting," Paula said over her coffee mug.

"Yes, but if you really want to be bold, why not get Chase something that would really stand out?"

"Such as?" Paula wondered.

"A diamond ring for Christmas," Monica replied.

"What?" Paula's mouth hung open.

"Sure, why not? Yes, I know he's a diamond jeweler, but Chase hasn't worn jewelry since he removed his wedding ring. I have a feeling he'd be honored to wear a ring that you gave him."

"I'm not so sure about that," Paula sighed. She wondered if Chase might feel it was akin to an engagement ring, making him nervous. He might even feel pressured to give her an engagement ring earlier than he planned, if that was his plan. Could be that he wasn't even looking to replace his wedding band anytime soon.

Monica seemed to read her mind. "Don't worry about attaching any special significance to it. Just giving him the ring will speak for itself as a gift of appreciation for what he means to you. As for cost, we have some great rings that won't break the bank, but are priceless to the recipient."

An ingenuous smile played on Paula's mouth. Maybe this was the ideal gift for the ideal man. She liked the thought of Chase wearing a diamond band as her Christmas gift for him to enjoy, no matter what the future held for them.

"I'm starting to warm up to the idea in a hurry," she told Monica.

"Good for you." Monica gave her an enthusiastic smile. "And even better for Chase."

Paula couldn't agree more as she contemplated picking out the perfect ring.

Chase entered the diamond store bearing his surname. He had come to the conclusion that it was time to ask Paula to marry him. He pulled the engagement ring that Isabelle had given him out of his pocket. It was white gold with several small diamonds and sapphires. The ring had lost much of its luster and would need a slight adjustment in size. Most importantly, Chase wanted a center stone that would make Paula take notice, sweep her off her sexy feet and make it impossible for her to say no.

He walked to the counter where Zachary was working. Last he'd heard, Monica was still sweet on the man. Chase waited for him to finish with a customer before proceeding with something his heart said was the right thing to do and the right time.

"Here to check up on us?" joked Zachary.

Chase smiled. "Not this time." He set the engagement ring on the counter for his gemologist to examine.

"What have we here?" Zachary asked.

"It belongs to Paula's grandmother," Chase told him.

"Nice."

"She's entrusted me with it to ask for her granddaughter's hand in marriage," Chase explained.

Zachary flashed a broad smile. "Congratulations!"

Chase grinned. "Thanks."

"So, Paula's ready to make an honest man out of you?"

"I think it's more the other way around," Chase replied, knowing that he really wanted Paula to be his wife.

Zachary picked up the ring and studied it. "It's definitely an antique."

"Yeah, it is. I'd like to have it cleaned and polished, and then I want to add a few more diamonds, including a nice center stone."

"Well, you've come to the right place. But I'm sure I don't have to convince you of that," Zachary said with a sly grin on his lips.

Chase chuckled. "Not at all."

"Why don't we take a look at some stones that have your future bride's name written all over them?" Zachary suggested.

Chase liked the sound of that. Referring to Paula as his new wife was even more exciting to look forward to. "Yes, why don't we take a look," he directed his employee.

It didn't take long for Chase to choose some diamonds that seemed to epitomize exactly what he was looking for. He wanted to remain true to Isabelle's original ring as much as possible. It was equally important to Chase that he give Paula a ring that wasn't too gaudy, yet clearly illustrated his love and commitment to a long relationship with her. He chose a two-carat radiant-cut diamond as the centerpiece. The stone beguiled Chase, even though he was used to seeing exceptional diamonds.

"That's a real beaut." Zachary whistled. "No woman would be able to resist it, or the man giving it to her."

Chase smiled. He wasn't interested in any woman, only

Paula. Having her accept his offer of marriage would be a dream come true. With the rich personal and professional ties he had, Paula in his life was like icing on the cake. "I'll need it ready by Saturday," he said thoughtfully. "I'm having a party and plan to make my move there."

"Not a problem." Zachary looked at Chase. "I hope I'm invited to this party?"

"Absolutely. I assume you'll be bringing Monica?" Knowing she would definitely be there, Chase didn't want it to be too awkward if things had cooled off with them.

"Oh, yeah. She'll be right on my arm and probably getting a few ideas of her own about marriage."

Chase grinned. "If it's meant to be, I'm sure you two can make whatever future you want."

"That's true." Zachary tilted his head. "Good luck on Saturday."

"I never like to depend on luck for anything. Better to put my faith in Paula that she'll want me as much as I do her."

"I am so proud of you both," Isabelle told Paula during the drive to Chase's house. "Anyone can see that you're wild about each other."

Beaming, Paula glanced over at her. "That's because we are." She was quick to acknowledge how much they were into each other, particularly to the one person who had always been able to read her like a book. "And it doesn't matter if others see it or not, only those we care about. For me, that starts with you."

Now it was Isabelle's turn to beam. "I've seen it practically from the very beginning, child."

"So you say," Paula teased.

"I knew it was only a matter of time before you both saw it, too."

"I guess you were right about that," Paula said with amusement. "We've definitely come around."

Isabelle drew a breath. "I don't want to jinx things, but I

have a feeling that it won't be too long before Chase pops the question."

Paula had the same feeling. "Let's just wait until it happens," she said cautiously. "I know Chase loves me, and that's what's most important for now."

Isabelle studied her. "I agree, but it doesn't mean it won't progress to the next level and the one after that. When a man gives you a diamond pendant, it's his way of telling you he's very serious about the relationship."

"I'm sure he is." Paula changed lanes. "Right now, I just want to have a good time at the party and see what the New Year brings."

As long as we're together, anything is possible.

"Excuse me, but aren't you forgetting something?" Isabelle uttered.

"What am I forgetting, Isa?"

"Before we get to the New Year, Christmas comes first," Isabelle reminded her. "And who knows what Santa might have in store for you."

Paula grinned. "You're right about that."

"A grandmother definitely knows best." Isabelle chuckled.

Paula had always loved Christmastime, and this year would certainly be no exception. Chase had proven to be the greatest gift of all. Anything else would be an added blessing. She considered the prospect of receiving an engagement ring from Chase and how special that would make her feel. Paula hoped the same would be true for him when she gave him the ring she'd picked out for his Christmas present.

Chase greeted Isabelle with a kiss on the cheek, followed by kissing Paula on the mouth. He noticed she was holding a covered platter. "What's this?" he asked.

"Oh, Isa insisted on making some oatmeal-and-chocolate-chip cookies for the party," Paula said.

Chase smiled at Isabelle. "Thanks, I appreciate your thoughtfulness. Judging by your cooking that I've already had the pleasure of tasting, I'm sure they're delicious."

Isabelle's eyes crinkled. "I was only too happy to do my part."

"Let me take your coats," Chase said.

They handed their coats to him, and he tossed them over his outstretched arm. He admired Paula in a striking, sexy, black halter dress.

"You look lovely," he told her.

"Thank you. You're looking pretty spiffy yourself." Paula grinned and gave him the once-over. He was wearing a dark brown sport coat over a black polo sweater and brown pants.

"Flattery will get you everywhere," he joked.

"I'm counting on it," she retorted.

He laughed. "You're the first guests to arrive. Why don't you put the cookies in the kitchen while I hang up your coats?"

Chase hung the coats in a closet and made room for others. He felt a trifle nervous, knowing that later he would be proposing to Paula in front of family and friends. He expected her to say yes, but it still didn't prevent his heart from thumping wildly like a drum. The sooner they got that part out of the way, the sooner the rest of the party could be enjoyed.

When he returned, Chase found Paula and Isa in the great room, no doubt admiring Paula's handiwork. Nat King Cole's classic "The Christmas Song" was playing softly in the background.

"Can I get anyone a drink?" he asked. "I've got eggnog, wine, beer, brandy, soda…"

"Slow down, baby," Paula said. She slid her arm around his waist. "Remember, we're cohosting this party, so let us help you. And that starts with us getting our own drinks, thank you."

"Of course." Chase grinned sheepishly, welcoming the assistance from Paula and Isabelle. "Ladies, make yourselves at home and feel free to pitch in with whatever you want to do to help out."

"That's more like it," Isabelle said, giving him the eye before heading toward the kitchen.

Paula kissed him. Chase's lips lingered on hers until she gently pulled away. "We can pick that up later," she promised. "Right now, let's get ready to party!"

"Here's a little secret," he told her. "The party actually began the moment you arrived."

"Ohh," Paula batted her eyes lovingly, "that's so cute." She gave him another kiss. "Now let's hold off with the compliments. Otherwise, the kisses may never stop coming."

"Is that a promise?" Chase joked, restraining himself from going for more. "Don't answer that. We have guests arriving shortly."

He admired Paula's beauty and soul while thinking he couldn't wait to make her his wife.

Chapter 21

"This is Gail," Chase said to Paula. "She's working on her graduate gemologist degree while interning with us."

"Hi." Paula briefly scanned the tall, slender young woman with a stylish layered bob. Then her eyes darted to the man beside Gail, commanding more of Paula's attention, though she wished that hadn't been the case. It was her ex-beau, Sheldon Burke. What the hell was he doing there?

"This is Sheldon," Gail told Chase.

The two men shook hands.

"I hope you don't mind my crashing your party?" Sheldon said to Chase, seemingly going out of his way to avoid Paula's eyes.

"Not at all," Chase said in a friendly voice. "The more, the merrier. Besides, you're here with Gail. That's fine by me."

"Thanks, I appreciate it." Sheldon faced Paula. "It's nice to see you again."

Chase met her eyes. "You two know each other?"

"A-actually…" she stammered, fearful of what type of sick game Sheldon might be playing.

"We used to hang out," Sheldon said tersely. "No big deal."

"I see," Chase said thoughtfully, regarding him. "Well, welcome to my home, and feel free to circulate. Drinks are in the great room."

"We'll find them." Sheldon grinned. "C'mon, baby, let's circulate like the man said."

Paula watched Sheldon and Gail walk off holding hands, before facing Chase uneasily. She'd expected him to display jealousy or maybe admonish her for not talking much about her ex.

Instead, Chase flashed a smile. "Seems like a nice guy Gail has latched on to."

"He can be when he wants to," Paula said, leaving it at that. She preferred not to dwell on the near-stalker side of Sheldon, who had trouble leaving well enough alone. She hoped that was now truly a thing of the past.

Chase put his arm around her. "Well, that's between them. I'm happy with the woman I've chosen to be with."

Paula beamed. "I feel the same way about you," she assured him. He kissed her, and she wiped lip gloss from his mouth. "We'd better get back in there before people start to miss the hosts."

"You're right. We wouldn't want that, although I'm more interested in being alone with you later." Chase grinned seductively.

"Me, too," Paula said. She was looking forward to Sheldon leaving without making a scene. She wished Chase hadn't encouraged him to drink, knowing that his tendency to overdo it could spell trouble.

Chase danced with Paula to some Christmas music, enjoying the way she moved with such grace. He noted that Sheldon and Gail were dancing, too, though Sheldon seemed more interested in Paula. Or was that Chase's imagination?

He wasn't prone to imagining things. The man was definitely eyeing Paula, who didn't seem to notice. Neither did Gail. Chase considered that was a good thing on both counts, unless he began to see the women become uncomfortable.

He assumed Sheldon was one of Paula's old boyfriends. Chase had no problem with this. After all, he hadn't expected Paula to be a nun when they met. Most important was that she had put the past behind her, and so had he. If so, why did he suddenly feel that her past was not quite finished?

After the song ended, Virginia approached them. "Chase, can I borrow Paula for a minute?"

He gave her a brief smile. "Sure, but anything more than that and I'll come looking for you."

Virginia laughed. "I love him."

"Don't even think about it," Paula said, playfully giving Virginia the evil eye.

"As a friend," Virginia stated. "Plus, I see one or two men here who seem to be single. I just might go after one of them."

"Give it your best shot," Chase said. He watched as they headed off and then turned his gaze toward Sheldon. Gail was nowhere to be found. Sheldon seemed to be preoccupied with him. Chase wondered if it wasn't the other way around.

"Son," Sylvester said to Chase.

Chase turned to look at him. "Hi."

Sylvester was holding two drinks and handed Chase one. "Hell of a party you've got going here."

"I'm glad you think so." Chase was satisfied with the turnout that included a few friends, some neighbors, people from work and those Paula had invited.

"I may have picked up a new customer or two," Sylvester said enthusiastically.

"That's great to hear, Dad." Chase locked eyes with Sheldon.

Sylvester noticed. "What's going on?"

"I'll let you know when I find out," Chase responded. "Will you excuse me for a minute?"

He didn't wait for a reply, instead walking over to Sheldon.

Even then, Chase had no idea what he'd say, if anything. Only that he sensed the man had something to say to him. He might as well find out what it is.

"What's up?" Sheldon asked tonelessly.

"Just trying to be a good host," Chase said, wondering if he should back off right now.

"Yeah, I'll bet," Sheldon scoffed.

Chase's brows knitted. "Is there something you want to say to me now that you've got my full attention without the ladies present?"

Sheldon curled his lip. "What gives you that idea?"

"You tell me."

Sheldon rolled his eyes. "I heard that you and Paula are tight."

"We're seeing each other," Chase acknowledged stiffly. "Is that a problem?"

"Not with me," Sheldon said with a cold edge to his voice.

"You're sure about that?"

"Yeah, I'm sure." Sheldon sucked in a deep breath, circling the room with his eyes before they landed back on Chase. "Gail mentioned that you'd had this room redecorated."

"That's right." Chase wanted to give him the benefit of the doubt, but had a feeling there was more going on here than a battle of strong wills.

"I'll bet you hired Paula to do the job, right?"

Chase saw no reason to deny it. "Yes," he said unapologetically.

Sheldon ran his hand across his mouth. "Why am I not surprised?"

"Is there a point to any of this?" He was beginning to lose his patience.

"Yeah, there is." Sheldon spoke brusquely. "I hired her to fix up a room in my house. Then we started dating." He drew a breath. "I made the mistake of falling in love with her like you have. I can see it in your eyes."

Chase frowned, not sure he liked the implication. "Look, I'm sorry things didn't work out for you and Paula, but—"

"You should be sorry," Sheldon cut him off. "That's her pattern. Love 'em and leave 'em. If you're smart, you'll dump her before she dumps you just as soon as the next hot dude who needs an interior decorator comes along."

"I think I've heard all I want to," Chase spat, wishing it hadn't left such a bad taste in his mouth. "I also think it's time for you to leave my house."

"Sure, whatever you say." Sheldon's nostrils flared. "I know the truth hurts, man. I had to learn the hard way. I'm just passing on that wisdom before you get too involved, only to wish to hell you'd seen her for what she really is."

Chase bit his lip, watching as Sheldon went to talk to Gail. It was too late to turn back the clock now, as he had fallen in love with Paula for better or worse. Right now, it seemed to be for worse, as Chase wrestled with the implications of Sheldon's parting words.

"What is he doing here?" Virginia asked with irritation.

Paula gulped as they gazed at Sheldon, a smug grin on his face. He'd just chatted with Chase, and Paula could only imagine what Sheldon had said to him about her.

"He came with someone who works for Chase," she told Virginia. "I guess they're dating."

"And we're supposed to believe this was purely coincidental?"

"Why not?" Paula tried to take the high road. "We both thought Sheldon had moved on, remember?"

"Yes, and I still want to believe that," Virginia said. "But seeing him here of all places and talking to Chase like they're buddies scares me."

"I'm not too comfortable with it, either," Paula confessed. "But the worst thing I could do is confront Sheldon, or ask him to leave when he's here with Chase's blessing as Gail's date."

"I'll go talk to him," Virginia said. "We can't have Sheldon ruin the party."

"I'm afraid it may be too late for that," Chase said as he came up behind Paula.

"Chase," Paula said, facing his eyes that were so hard it nearly caused her to take a step back.

"I just had a very interesting conversation with your ex," he said sullenly.

Paula flinched. "What did he say to you?" she asked fearfully.

"Whatever it was," Virginia broke in, "don't let Sheldon get in your head, Chase. That man would say anything if it meant hurting Paula."

"I can speak for myself," Paula said firmly, appreciating Virginia coming to her defense. If there were issues on the table regarding her past, she had to clear them up herself and hope Chase would listen. She looked up at his face. It was as tense as she'd ever seen it, suggesting their relationship had been called into question. "Talk to me, baby."

"Not here," he said irritably. "Let's go upstairs."

"Okay." Paula looked at Virginia.

"Go ahead," she said. "I'll help Isa keep the party running smoothly till you guys get back."

Paula met Chase's gaze and wondered if the party was over.

Chase could barely wait till they were alone to confront Paula. He didn't want to believe that she had led him astray and couldn't be counted on to hold up her end of the bargain when all was said and done. Yet that's exactly what Sheldon had implied, though Chase had little doubt that the man was a vindictive bastard. That didn't mean there wasn't some truth in his words, cutting as they were.

Chase closed the door to his bedroom after Paula was inside. He studied her for a moment, trying to figure out just how well he knew the woman whom he'd been prepared to ask to marry him tonight. Maybe he didn't know her very well at all. Maybe she wasn't really in love with him the way he needed her to be in order for this work.

"Is it true that he was one of your clients before you hooked up with him?" Chase asked bluntly.

Paula seemed to fumble with her thoughts. "Yes," she said at last. "Sheldon hired me to redecorate his breakfast room. He asked me out later, and I said yes. We ended up dating for a short while, until I realized he wasn't what I was looking for."

Chase cocked a brow. "So this is a pattern with you? You romance men who hire you and then move on when things get too serious?"

"It's not like that," Paula insisted, frowning. "I never set out to have a romance with Sheldon. It just happened, and he soured when I got out. That's normal and has nothing to do with how I feel about you."

"That's not the way I see it." Chase sighed. "Seems to me you're not really sure how you feel. I don't know if it's something about eligible men you work for and becoming attached to, or a fear of commitment when it comes down to the nitty-gritty."

"I don't need to be psychoanalyzed about how I feel," Paula said, her lips tightly drawn. "I haven't made a habit of attaching myself to single clients, and I don't fear commitment to the right man—you."

Chase was less than convinced, going against his strongest desires. "How do I know you aren't just telling me what I want to hear?" he questioned.

"You'll just have to trust me on that," she responded tersely. "I don't take such words lightly."

He bristled. "Trust you, huh? Should I really? Did you ever consider Sheldon to be the 'right man,' before unceremoniously ending things with him?"

Paula glared at Chase through watered eyes. "I never told Sheldon I loved him, if that's what you're wondering. I would *only* say that to a man if I really meant it." She slowly put her arms around Chase's waist. "Can't you see that Sheldon's simply trying to drive a wedge between us as payback because his ego couldn't handle being dumped?"

Chase didn't doubt that for one second. He knew how men got when trying to deal with rejection, especially when they were in love with the woman. It was similar to losing a loved one through death. He could understand how Sheldon wanted to strike back when the opportunity presented itself, but that didn't make it right. Chase didn't want to feed off the man's parting shot, but he couldn't deny that it had had an effect on him, whether he wanted it to or not.

He closed his eyes, allowing Paula to continue holding him while refraining from doing the same. He could feel her heart beating rapidly. The closeness between them reminded Chase of why he had fallen in love with Paula. He wished with all his heart that they could just put everything in their pasts behind them and live happily thereafter. But this was the real world, and he needed to reassess their relationship before things went any further and he wound up making the biggest mistake of his life.

Chase moved away from Paula, favoring her with a bleak stare. "Look, I think we need to take a step back."

Her eyes widened. "What are you saying?"

He looked away. "Things are moving too fast between us."

"If this is about—"

"It has nothing to do with your ex," Chase said, trying to convince her if not himself, "other than it made me realize that I'm not ready to take this to the next level yet." He forced himself to meet her eyes. "If you decide to break things off, I'll understand."

"I love you," Paula said, her eyes watering. "I don't want to break things off. You mean too much to me. If you're getting cold feet about our relationship for whatever reason, just say so."

Chase wanted to back down and carry on with the evening as planned. He checked himself from succumbing to emotions, believing it wouldn't be fair to either of them to pretend that doubts had not surfaced, real or imagined.

"My feelings about you haven't changed," he told her

candidly. "Let's just give this some time and see how things go. Are you willing to do that?"

"Whatever you want." Paula dabbed at her eyes. "When you realize that there's nothing phony about what I feel for you, give me a call."

Chase felt a chill as Paula peered at him before marching out of the bedroom. He stood there for a moment, wondering if he had unwittingly sabotaged their relationship, or if he'd just suspended a marriage that he'd thought was inevitable. Chase took the box out of his pocket, opened it and regarded Isabelle's customized engagement ring that he had planned to give Paula tonight with family and friends surrounding them. Now he had to wonder if it would ever happen.

Chapter 22

"Call him," Isabelle urged Paula, the sternness in her voice clearly evident. "It's the only way to get things back on track with Chase."

"I can't," Paula said stubbornly a week after Chase's party had ended on a dour note. It was the last time they had spoken, and she was frustrated that Chase had chosen not to call. She feared that the relationship they had carefully built was slowly slipping away.

"And why not?" Isabelle's eyes narrowed as Paula lay in bed feeling sorry for herself.

"Because I'm not the one who decided to slow things down," she said snappily. "Chase has my number and can call me anytime he wants."

"I know that, but sometimes you have to be the bigger person. Moping around the house isn't the answer, not when it's as plain as the nose on your face that you still love Chase."

"I never said I didn't," Paula said emotionally. "I've never been more in love. But how can I fight back when Sheldon has him believing that I'm only interested in short-term relationships with men I work for? That couldn't be further from the truth, but Chase apparently has enough doubts now that he's willing to set aside everything, even though it should be perfectly clear that I want to spend the rest of my life with him."

"You can't allow your life to be dictated by a bitter ex!" Isabelle's brows drew together. "Maybe he did get to Chase. Or maybe Chase was just a bit scared of his own feelings and needed to be reassured that you truly were in this for the long haul. Either way, this is your future we're talking about. Don't throw it away because of pride. Chase is too good of a catch to let him slip through your fingers, even if you have to make the first move to patch things up."

Paula wanted to bury her head under the pillow. But that would only deprive her of air, not the feelings she had for Chase, which weren't going away anytime soon, if ever. The truth was, she hadn't been able to eat, drink, work or sleep since their confrontation. Though part of Paula believed this was proof that she was destined to remain single and unhappy all her life, the better part of her refused to succumb to that notion. What she had with Chase was real, even if he was faltering. They were meant to be together as sure as anyone ever had been. If Chase couldn't see this on his own, she had to reach out to him and try to hold on to her man and the promise of a future with him.

Paula managed to smile at her grandmother, who clearly wasn't about to take no for an answer. "All right, all right, I'll call him. Satisfied?"

"Not till I know you two are back together where you belong," Isabelle said firmly. A hint of a smile played on her lips. "One step at a time."

"Agreed."

Isabelle reached into her pocket. "I brought this up, thinking you might need it."

Paula grinned as she took the cell phone. "Thanks, Isa. You think of everything."

"That's what grandmothers do. We want to make things better for our grandchildren, especially at this time of year."

Paula had practically forgotten that Christmas was only days away, so caught up was she in the way things had gone downhill between her and Chase. She waited till Isa had given her some privacy and then punched Chase's preprogrammed number before she could chicken out. Butterflies swarmed in Paula's stomach as she tried to think of what to say and what not to. She didn't want to blow this or give Chase further reason to doubt her love for him.

She got his voice mail. Paula hesitated, not wanting to talk to a machine in lieu of the man she loved. She hung up without leaving a message and pondered her next move to win Chase back.

Chase was at the Prince Club with his father for some man-to-man talk, even if he wasn't exactly in the mood for being lectured. Or maybe that was exactly what he needed— the voice of reason from someone who had been there. Chase was still vacillating back and forth about Paula and their relationship days after he'd all but accused her of playing with his emotions. His love for her was as strong as ever, but his confidence that they were right for each other had taken a hit. He wasn't interested in going from widower to being engaged to someone who might never make it to the altar once she realized it meant the end of being single to go after the next man who captured her attention. Was he being totally unfair to Paula based solely on the seed her bitter and inebriated ex had planted?

"Chase…?" Sylvester was saying.

He looked up from the fog he'd been in, not sure what had just been said. "I'm sorry," Chase said. "I drifted off for a moment there."

"I can see that." Sylvester gazed at him sharply. "What I said is you've got to get out of this funk. It's not you, son."

"I'm not sure about that." Chase lifted his drink. "Maybe

what you see is what you get, someone who's afraid of being hurt. After Rochelle's death, I don't think I can take another major blow to my love life. Yes, I know that Rochelle never meant to leave me, but she still did, just like Mom left you. The grief subsides, but it never fully goes away. It would be almost as unbearable if I were to pour my affections into a relationship with someone who was not totally on the same page but hoped to make me think otherwise till ready to step aside."

"I hear you," Sylvester said understandingly. "I just don't believe you have anything to worry about with Paula. She's the real thing, and I know she loves you just as much as you love her. Deep down inside, I think you know that, too."

"What I know is that she's been single all her life," Chase said stubbornly, even if conceding that he was largely blowing off steam in trying to make himself feel better and convinced that Paula really did love him and wanted to be with him. "Maybe there's a reason for that. Can I really ask someone to marry me who may not have being single out of her system? What if Paula says yes and then on her next redecorating job she meets someone richer and better-looking than me? Could that spell the end of our relationship?"

Sylvester furrowed his brow. "I don't think so. Listen to me. Paula's not a gold digger. I have no idea why it didn't work out between her and this other fella, but their relationship has nothing to do with you."

"You're sure about that?" Chase asked with reservations. "When I first met Paula, she practically jumped down my throat for just looking at her. Maybe there was an underlying theme there that was saying don't get involved with me or I'll only end up breaking your heart."

Sylvester shook his head and sipped his cocktail. "Will you listen to yourself? You don't believe that any more than I do. I had a good feeling about Paula from the start, which is why I sent her your way. I've seen nothing to make me doubt my initial instincts. The reason some people stay single is that they can't find someone worthy of getting involved with for a lifetime. Paula found that with you, just as you have with her. Don't throw it all away for no good reason."

"So you think I'm being foolish by having second thoughts about us?" Chase asked, studying his drink.

"No, I wouldn't say foolish. More like overly cautious and not giving yourself enough credit for recognizing what you see in Paula," Sylvester said.

Chase conceded that he saw a lot in her to admire and fall in love with. He just questioned whether or not it was enough to eliminate all doubts. He didn't want to jump back in only to jump out again when the going got tough. That was no way to go into an engagement, let alone marriage. Was it wrong to want someone he could count on no matter what for as long as they lived?

"If you're asking me if there are guarantees for what might or might not happen down the line, I'd say no," Sylvester voiced, seeming to read Chase's mind. "None of us knows what the future holds, but if you want your crusty old man's opinion about what chance you and Paula have for a long and happy relationship, I'd say it's a damned strong likelihood. You just need to lighten up and go with your heart on this one, son."

Chase put the drink to his lips thoughtfully. His heart was the most important thing he had going for him. It did belong to Paula, whether he wanted to admit that or not. Having his heart broken was not an option any more than he would ever knowingly break her heart. Maybe they could rekindle the flames without missing a beat and put the weight of the world behind them.

Chase had wanted to call Paula on more than one occasion but wasn't sure what to say. He was aware that Paula had called him today, but she didn't leave a message. Did that suggest she was also at a loss for the proper words, or had she acquiesced to his desire to slow things down? Maybe she was fine with them keeping their distance, or maybe the whole thing was tearing her apart as it was him.

Chase homed in on his father's eyes that were already peering at him. "You think I need to go with my heart, huh?"

Sylvester nodded. "It trumps pretty much everything else when it comes to knowing what's right and wrong concerning love. I have complete faith that you'll get beyond your misgivings and apprehension and give Paula the chance to prove her love is every bit as strong as yours. She deserves that. Once you realize the truth, there will be no stopping you two from getting the most out of your relationship."

Chase cracked a smile. "Thanks for listening."

"I think it was more the other way around, don't you?" Sylvester asked.

Chase chuckled. "Yeah, I guess you have been doing most of the talking. I've absorbed it all, and, as always, you've managed to put things in a proper perspective for me."

Sylvester patted him on the arm warmly. "If I can't pass on to you some of what I've learned about life, I haven't been a very good father."

"You've been great," Chase made clear, especially with his real mother out of the picture. "I wouldn't have wanted anyone else."

Sylvester's eyes crinkled. "I feel the same way about you, son." He stood. "Right now, I have to run to the men's room. Why don't you order us one more round, then we'll get out of here."

"Okay, sounds good." Chase watched him disappear. He mused about Paula, regretting the way he'd reacted to Sheldon's cutting words. Chase also felt it had been a good chance to reconsider their relationship, which had been hot and heavy, before making any moves that could very well have implications for the rest of their lives.

Two days before Christmas, Paula was jogging with Virginia. They weren't bothered by the light snow that was falling and sticking to the ground, or the cold temperature. Having not heard from Chase since his party, Paula decided she would show up on his doorstep on Christmas Day. It was the right thing to do, if only to show him she still cared and hoped he did, too. She was perfectly willing to start over if that's what he wanted. However, some things could not be easily erased from her memory, such as their steamy, passionate lovemaking that Paula sorely missed.

"I think that's a terrific idea," Virginia said when Paula told her what her plan was.

Paula looked over at her. "You don't think it would be encroaching on Chase's territory against his wishes, do you?"

Virginia shook her head. "The man didn't say he never wanted to see you again. What better time to get things going again than on Christmas Day?"

"But he's never bothered to call me," Paula complained. "I miss him like crazy, but maybe he doesn't miss me."

Virginia rolled her eyes. "You haven't called him, either, may I remind you. Does that mean you've stopped caring?"

"No, but I did try to call him once. When I got his voice mail, I hung up." Paula frowned. "At least he would have seen that I called."

"Yeah, but you didn't leave a message, so it doesn't count."

"I didn't want to sound desperate or like I was some kind of stalker," Paula suggested, though she knew that sounded lame.

"Oh, please, girl!" Virginia said. "I'm sure that whatever Chase thinks of you, he'd never believe you were desperate or a stalker. It's obvious that you could have any man out there you wanted, yet you chose Chase even after he flaked out on you. That should tell him something."

"He didn't flake out." Paula quickly came to his defense. "Sheldon got exactly what he wanted, the chance to make me look bad in Chase's eyes. Chase only reacted the way anyone would have by questioning if I was really in this for the right reasons. I should've done a better job convincing him how much I love him."

"I think you did a great job of that," Virginia said. "Don't put this on yourself. Chase has to know that you're anything but a phony. You can't help but show the real you. I'm sure that when you see Chase on Christmas, he'll understand and not give you a chance to back out the door."

Paula could only hope she was right. She didn't even want to think about ringing in the New Year without Chase. Anything less would be unbearable. He held the key to her heart; she couldn't imagine anyone ever being able to take his place.

On Christmas Eve, Chase went to the cemetery to visit Rochelle's grave. He had done this for the last two years, wanting to be with her in spirit at a time that was once so important in their lives. Also, this time he wanted to let her know that the torch had been passed to another woman as wonderful as she was. He was sure that Rochelle was up there rooting for him and Paula to be as happy as they had been.

After saying his piece, Chase laid three long-stemmed yellow roses against her headstone. They were Rochelle's favorite flower. He heard some rustling, and Chase turned around to find Monica standing there.

"Hey," he said.

"Your dad told me I'd find you here," she said softly.

"Yeah." Chase glanced at Rochelle's headstone. "I needed to come here."

"I know." Monica met his eyes. "She understands."

He nodded. "Thanks for coming."

"That's what friends are for." She paused. "Next time you can bring someone even closer to you."

"I'm not sure—"

"It's okay," Monica said. "I believe Paula can handle these things. No matter what happens with you two, she wants to be a part of every aspect of your life, and that includes supporting you when you visit Rochelle's grave."

Chase's eyes watered. "That's good to know." He would surely need that kind of support from the woman he loved.

"Let me buy you a cup of coffee, and we can talk about the New Year's Eve party we're giving."

"I'd like that," he said. "But Christmas comes first, and I've got some plans of my own."

"Oh, really?" Monica's eyes opened wide. "I'd love to hear all about them."

"Then you will."

Chase immediately turned his thoughts to Paula and what he had in mind for her Christmas gift.

Chapter 23

Paula helped Isabelle make a sweet-potato pie. It had been their Christmas Day ritual ever since she was a little girl, and Paula enjoyed the bonding experience. She hoped to pass it on to her children someday. Would Chase be their father? Paula got a warm feeling at the thought. They could be a happy family, if only Chase would open up his heart to her again and allow their love to blossom.

Maybe when I visit him later today, we'll patch things up and start over.

"How are those potatoes coming along?" Isabelle asked as she rolled out the crust.

"They're almost ready," Paula said, checking them with a fork.

"Good. Together we'll make this a perfect dessert on this day of blessings."

Paula eyed her with a raised brow. "Do you know something I don't?"

Isabelle smiled. "Not that I'm aware of. What I do know

is that Christmas is a true blessing in and of itself. If you believe in the spirit of it, then you know anything is possible."

"You mean like Chase and me getting back together?"

"Every couple has bumps in the road, child. It's no different with you and Chase. The man loves you, and you love him. Sheldon's vengefulness and immaturity can't change that."

"I love your optimism." How could she not? After all, Isa had passed much of that on to her in every aspect of her life.

"It's up to you and Chase to work things out," Isabelle said, putting the plated pie crust in the refrigerator to chill. "The fact that you're planning to see him this afternoon will go a long way in that regard."

"And what if it doesn't?" asked Paula. "I don't want to make a fool out of myself."

"You could never do that. Chase may be stubborn just like you, but he'll respect that you're reaching out to him. All it will take is him looking in your eyes to know that he's the love you've sought all your life."

Paula walked over and hugged her. "And you're the best grandmother anyone could ever have."

"I'll hold you to that." Isabelle kissed her cheek. "Now, let's finish up this pie so we can go open us some gifts before folks start to drop by."

Paula flashed her teeth. "One pie coming right up!"

They heard the bell ring.

"Looks like company's already here," Isabelle said.

"I'll get it, Paula said, drying her hands. "It's probably just Virginia coming by to see what I thought of her gift."

She opened the door and was startled to see Chase standing there. He had on a topcoat and was holding two gift-wrapped boxes.

Chase gazed at Paula as she stood in the doorway. She was as beautiful as ever, like an angel sent back to earth to rescue him. The sparkle in her eyes told him all he needed to know. He wondered how he could have ever doubted her.

"Hello," he said, clearing his throat.

"Hi." Her voice shook.

"Can I come in?"

She stepped aside.

Chase walked through the foyer into the living room. He saw the Christmas tree decorated and lit, with a generous amount of gifts around it. His nose picked up the scent of fresh coffee. He faced Paula. "I wanted to call, but…"

"It's okay," she said graciously.

Chase didn't necessarily agree, wishing he had picked up the phone just once. "I needed to do some soul-searching."

Paula favored him with a toothless smile. "I understand."

Isabelle came in from the kitchen. "Merry Christmas," she told Chase sprightly.

"Merry Christmas, Isa," he said and held out the bigger box. "This is for you."

She took it, gushing, "You shouldn't have."

"I wanted to get you something. When I saw it at the mall, I felt it was the perfect gift for you. Hope you like it."

"Do you want me to open it now?" she asked.

"That's not necessary." Chase glanced at the tree. "I think you have some other gifts that should be opened first."

"All right," Isabelle said. "I'll leave you two alone."

"No, stay," he requested and turned to Paula. "Here's your gift." He gave her the small box. "You can open yours now."

Paula gazed at him thoughtfully, sighed and pulled off the ribbon. She meticulously tore off the gift wrap, revealing a white box. Chase felt his heart rate speed up, knowing this moment would change everything forever between them.

Taking the lid off, Paula saw a batch of uncut diamonds of different shapes, sizes and color. She put her hand inside and pulled out a diamond ring. She gazed up at Chase wide-eyed.

He took the ring from her. "Look familiar?"

Paula gasped and looked over at Isabelle. "It's yours…"

"Not anymore, child," Isabelle said happily.

Chase connected with Isabelle's approving eyes and

nodded. It was time to make this official. He got down on one knee and took Paula's hand, placing the ring on her finger. It was a perfect fit.

"Paula, will you marry me?" Chase asked, keeping his tone steady even as he quivered inside.

Paula stared at the ring, enthralled, before looking down at Chase. "Oh, Chase…"

"Paula…" He drew in a deep breath. "It was something I'd planned to do before now, but things got in the way for a moment there. That's over now. I love you, Paula, and I want you to be my wife. If you'll do me the honor of allowing me to be your husband, I'll be the happiest man in the world."

Paula closed her eyes, squeezing out tears. When she opened them again, Chase knew he had his answer, but he still needed to hear the words.

"Yes," she uttered emphatically. "I'll marry you, Chase."

His own eyes watered. "Yeah?"

"Yes, yes, yes!" She knelt down next to him. "I love you, too, and I'd like nothing more than to become Mrs. Chase McCord!"

"Thank you." Chase wiped one of his cheeks. "Thank you, Isa, for providing the bridge between the past and future with your engagement ring."

"It was always Paula's birthright," she said proudly. "I'm delighted to see it passed on to another generation as a gift of love for your life together."

"I'll cherish it always," Paula cried.

"I know you will," Isabelle said affectionately. "Now that we've gotten the hard part out of the way, will you two please kiss to seal the deal?"

"There's no arguing with your grandmother," Chase said, happy to oblige. "Not on Christmas."

"I'm with you there," Paula agreed. "Grandmother definitely knows best!"

Chase held her cheeks and put their lips together for a nice kiss before getting to his feet. He pulled Paula up. "Why don't we try that again with less strain on our knees?"

She laughed. "It would be my pleasure. And something tells me that Isa would be the last person to object."

Isabelle beamed. "No objection here. Kiss away and let your love carry you both to new heights."

Chase doubted he could feel any higher than he did at the moment. He'd just become engaged to the beautiful woman he was prepared to spend the rest of his life with, and he was sure that Paula felt the same way.

As though to prove the point, this time she grabbed his cheeks, opened her mouth perfectly and passionately kissed Chase's lips. He reciprocated, and the kiss was everything Chase could have asked for and then some from his wife to be.

Paula could hardly believe that Isa had conspired with Chase in parting with her own diamond engagement ring. It meant more to Paula than she could ever say to be able to carry on the legacy started by her grandfather. Equally heartwarming was the realization that Chase had overcome all doubts in asking her to marry him with a box of glittering Christmas diamonds. Paula knew she had found the right man for her and vowed to be the best wife she possibly could for as long as they lived.

In the excitement of Chase's proposal and the sparkle in her grandmother's eyes as they all sat around the Christmas tree, Paula almost forgot that she'd also bought Chase a gift. This seemed like the perfect time to give it to him. She reached under the tree and grabbed a box.

"I have something for you," Paula said as Isa left them alone.

"What have we here?" Chase asked, eyeing the box.

"You'll have to open it to find out."

"Okay." He lifted the lid and saw the diamond ring. The shock on Chase's face was replaced by a broad grin. "You got me a ring?"

"Yes," Paula said, taking a breath. "It was something I thought would be a unique and unexpected gift for a man of diamonds. I hope you like it. Merry Christmas!"

Chase removed the ring and studied it. It was black titanium, with an eighteen-karat-gold inlay and a round diamond as the centerpiece.

"I love it!" he exclaimed. "But this must have cost you a fortune."

"Not really. I got a nice discount from a good friend of yours."

Chase nodded smilingly. He tried it on and stretched his hand, spreading the fingers. "Fits like a charm. How did you know we'd…?"

"I just did," Paula said. Never mind if her faith in the strength of their relationship had been tested. They had both passed the test at the end of the day. "Love has a way of always working itself out."

"I couldn't agree more," Chase uttered, a wide grin appearing on his face. He admired the ring again. "It's one of the best gifts anyone has ever given me for Christmas."

Paula beamed, gazing at her own sparkling engagement ring before meeting his eyes. "And you're definitely the very *best* gift I've ever gotten, period!"

"That so?"

"Yes, it is so, and I'll keep proving it to you time and time again."

Chase moistened his lips. "Why don't you start right now?"

"I'll be happy to."

Paula tilted her head and gave him a loving, passionate, Christmas kiss. She was in no hurry to pull their mouths apart anytime soon.

Ten years.
Eight grads.
One weekend.
The homecoming
of a lifetime.

PASSION OVERTIME

PAMELA YAYE

As homecoming festivities heat up, PR rep Kyra Dixon is assigned to nab pro football star Terrence Franklin as Hollington's new head coach. Kyra knows the sexy star well... intimately, in fact. Kyra and Terrence were once engaged... until he dumped her for football dreams of glory and groupies. Now they've got some unfinished business to resolve—the business of seduction.

Hollington Homecoming:
Where old friends reunite...
and new passions take flight.

HOLLINGTON HOMECOMING

KIMANI ROMANCE

Coming the first week of November 2009
wherever books are sold.

In December, look for book 4 of Hollington Homecoming,
Tender to His Touch by Adrianne Byrd.

www.kimanipress.com
www.myspace.com/kimanipress

KPPY1371109

'Tis the season for seduction....

Holiday *Kisses*

Essence bestselling author
Gwynne Forster

KIMANI ROMANCE

Gwynne Forster
ESSENCE BESTSELLING AUTHOR

Holiday *Kisses*

Kisha Moran knows next to nothing about Craig Jackson—which seems to be just the way the secretive TV-news anchor likes it, despite their undeniable chemistry. Craig is tired of celebrity-hunting women, but something tells him Kisha is different. So he's thoroughly confused when feisty Kisha goes ice-cold on *him*. Craig realizes that the only gift he wants this Christmas is another chance to show her the man behind the mystery....

> **"Gwynne Forster writes with a fresh, sophisticated sensuality."**
> —*RT Book Reviews*

Coming the first week of November 2009 wherever books are sold.

KIMANI™ ROMANCE

www.kimanipress.com
www.myspace.com/kimanipress

KPGF1361109

The art of seduction... amidst the portrait of desire.

PICTURE
PERFECT
Christmas

MELANIE SCHUSTER

Chastain Thibodaux is no longer the awkward, naive girl who had her heart broken by Philippe Devereaux. Now the successful artist has included three sensuous nudes of Philippe in her prestigious gallery show—all therapeutic memories of their smoldering affair. When Philippe arrives at the opening demanding an explanation, his anger mixes with desire. And he vows to have Chastain back where she belongs—in his arms.

"Top-notch romance with skillfully portrayed emotions."
—*RT Book Reviews* on
A Case for Romance

Coming the first week of November 2009 wherever books are sold.

www.kimanipress.com
www.myspace.com/kimanipress

KIMANI™
ROMANCE

KPMS1381109

REQUEST YOUR FREE BOOKS!

2 FREE NOVELS
PLUS 2 FREE GIFTS!

KIMANI™ ROMANCE

Love's ultimate destination!

YES! Please send me 2 FREE Kimani™ Romance novels and my 2 FREE gifts (gifts are worth about $10). After receiving them, if I don't wish to receive any more books, I can return the shipping statement marked "cancel." If I don't cancel, I will receive 4 brand-new novels every month and be billed just $4.69 per book in the U.S. or $5.24 per book in Canada. That's a savings of over 20% off the cover price. It's quite a bargain! Shipping and handling is just 50¢ per book.* I understand that accepting the 2 free books and gifts places me under no obligation to buy anything. I can always return a shipment and cancel at any time. Even if I never buy another book from Kimani Press, the two free books and gifts are mine to keep forever.

168 XDN EYQG   368 XDN EYQS

Name	(PLEASE PRINT)

Address	Apt. #

City	State/Prov.	Zip/Postal Code

Signature (if under 18, a parent or guardian must sign)

Mail to **The Reader Service:**
IN U.S.A.: P.O. Box 1867, Buffalo, NY 14240-1867
IN CANADA: P.O. Box 609, Fort Erie, Ontario L2A 5X3

Not valid to current subscribers of Kimani Romance books.

Want to try two free books from another line?
Call 1-800-873-8635 or visit www.morefreebooks.com.

* Terms and prices subject to change without notice. Prices do not include applicable taxes. Sales tax applicable in N.Y. Canadian residents will be charged applicable provincial taxes and GST. Offer not valid in Quebec. This offer is limited to one order per household. All orders subject to approval. Credit or debit balances in a customer's account(s) may be offset by any other outstanding balance owed by or to the customer. Please allow 4 to 6 weeks for delivery. Offer available while quantities last.

Your Privacy: Kimani Press is committed to protecting your privacy. Our Privacy Policy is available online at www.eHarlequin.com or upon request from the Reader Service. From time to time we make our lists of customers available to reputable third parties who may have a product or service of interest to you. If you would prefer we not share your name and address, please check here. ☐

KROM09